CREWSING

Life on the Ocean Wave

By

Mike Aylward

Published by New Generation Publishing in 2017

Copyright © Mike Aylward 2017

First Edition

The author asserts the moral right under the Copyright, Designs and Patents Act 1988 to be identified as the author of this work.

All Rights reserved. No part of this publication may be reproduced, stored in a retrieval system or transmitted, in any form or by any means without the prior consent of the author, nor be otherwise circulated in any form of binding or cover other than that which it is published and without a similar condition being imposed on the subsequent purchaser.

www.newgeneration-publishing.com

New Generation Publishing

This book is dedicated to the memory of my dearest mother, Isa, who was both my inspiration and my role model on how to conduct myself in life. Thank you, Mum, all my love always, and God Bless you.

FOREWORD

The Queen Mary was built by the John Brown Shipyard on the River Clyde, Glasgow, in Lanarkshire, Scotland, an interesting fact being that two of my uncles, on my mother's side, actually worked on building her. Her keel was laid on 1st December 1930 and she was launched on 26th September 1934. It then took a further twenty months to fit out the ship (including the hand painted murals that adorned most public rooms) and carry out her sea trials in readiness for her maiden voyage on 27th May 1936.She was the largest ship ever to have been built up until that date and weighed in at a colossal 81,237 gross tonnes (I would love to have seen the scales they used to weigh her!).

She was 1,020 feet long (twice the height of Beachy Head if you stood the ship up on its stern), 118 feet wide and 181 feet high (11 feet taller than Nelson's Column), over 10 million rivets were used in her construction, she had 12 decks, with over 2,000 portholes.

Her peacetime capacity was for 1,957 passengers, plus a full complement of 1,174 officers and crew, which included a full time gardener! Not only was this ship exceptionally large, but she was extremely fast with her 27 boilers producing some 160,000 horsepower, which drove her four huge propellers to a cruising speed of 28.5 knots (I never actually saw these and so I am not exactly sure just how big they were). Can you imagine driving your car along the road, and keeping below the speed limit of thirty mph and having an 81,237 tonnes of a ship almost able to keep pace with you, not to mention your surprise at seeing a ship alongside you on the road.

The Mary (as we affectionately called her) had two stabilisers which she was able to use in rough seas to counteract the force of the sea, which in turn minimised the discomfort for the passengers. Unfortunately, this slowed her speed down tremendously and consequently were only used in extremely rough seas. The Queen Mary held the Blue Ribbon for the fastest passenger ship's crossing the Atlantic, which she held for over fourteen years, between 1938 and 1952, when she lost this prestigious trophy to the SS United States, which reputedly went straight into dry dock to repair the damage caused on this crossing.

She was designed to be the flag ship of the Cunard Steam Ship Company, and as such, it was the most indulgent ship ever built, including the Titanic, which had been launched some twenty-four years earlier and had held this title previously. During her working career, the Queen Mary made 1,001 passenger crossings of the Atlantic, a record she still proudly holds, despite her retirement to Long Beach California.

CHAPTER ONE

BANG! The door slammed shut and I opened my eyes. It wasn't a dream; here I was in a strait jacket locked up in an Alcohol Dependency Unit in a Specialist Home.

The last thing I could remember was lying on some pavement with two policemen trying to lift me up and put me into a waiting ambulance, yet here I was not even 20 years of age; no job; badly burnt hands, and a drink problem… all of which was spiralling me down into the black chasm known as hell!

It was only two years ago when my life appeared to finally moving forward after two false starts.

It all began in 1961…

The first rays of dawn finally began to penetrate the gap in my bedroom curtains to bring to an end one of the longest nights I could remember since I was a young child awaiting the arrival of Father Christmas. This was the beginning of a day of great excitement, as the decision I made today could determine my whole future and possibly influence the rest of my life. The choices were simple; should I leave home and join the crew of the Queen Mary, or should I stay at home and continue to enjoy the security that family and friends would bring?

If I accepted the job of Student Cook on the ship, this experience would bring a whole new dimension to my career, and, the presence of such an illustrious name on my CV would open many doors in the future. However, I had left home before and it had not worked out, partly due to my inability to settle down and overcome my homesickness. I realised that I would have the possibility of returning home for the odd day every two weeks and that I would have a fortnight's leave every ten weeks, but I was still worried about the possibility of being homesick. Naturally, I was aware that this previous experience was some two years earlier and that I had matured somewhat in the meantime. However, here I was, six foot two inches tall, weighing all of ten stone when soaking wet and still not eighteen years old. Nevertheless, I was still full of trepidation at the prospect of once again making the wrong decision which could ultimately result in my returning home as a failure, yet again.

The alternative was a much safer option, namely, to stay at home with my family and friends in my current and stress-free job as a Head Chef in a small local hotel. This option had a lot of appeal as it was comfortable, but it had very limited career prospects. Furthermore, if I chose the safe option, I knew that it would have more immediate repercussions as it meant that I would not have to miss the East Sussex mid-week football cup final which was taking place that very afternoon. I was the club captain; my team, who were the red hot favourites to win, meant I was certain to win a medal if I stayed! Not that I was, or ever had been a "pot hunter".

At the end of the day, the reality of this option was that I could remain in my dead end job with no prospects for a progressive and successful career; I could also continue in a relationship with a girl with whom I felt comfortable, but with whom I had no real future; and finally, I would have the opportunity to fulfil a football ambition which had very little significance other than to boost my ego. Bearing in mind that when I left home the first time, it was to pursue a lifelong ambition of taking up a professional football apprenticeship with a leading First Division team in the West Midlands.

At the time, this really was a golden opportunity as half of the England team – including the National Captain – all played for this particular team, and if I had been successful at this club, who could tell, I could ultimately have gone on and even had a possibility of winning a cap for my country.

Unfortunately, this was not to be, as I gave up this opportunity after only eight weeks, mainly because I was not allowed to play in my favourite position, that of an old-fashioned centre forward, for which I thought I had been recruited (the manager thought my future was to play in defence as a left back, which I hated, especially as I could not kick a football with my left foot to save my life!). Also, I did not adjust to life in "digs", living with a strange family in the Black Country; the fact that I was having great difficulty in understanding the accent may have further influenced my decision (there goes any chance of selling any of my books in the Midlands!).

As you will have gathered, I had already mentally made my decision to go to sea, although I remained extremely nervous about what might lie ahead. That morning remains as fresh in my memory as if it was only yesterday; indeed I still remember having a cold water strip wash in the kitchen sink (we were not posh and did not have a shower and we certainly did not have running hot water.). I shaved, again in cold water, before getting dressed and, for the first time in my life, I was actually the first one up and downstairs, a feat I never achieved before or since, even in the days when I had a paper round, as my father used to wake me up! Obviously, this historic day was as much a shock to my family as it was to me, but here I was, and as this was my last day at home for some time, I decided to give everyone a real treat by giving them all a cup of tea in bed, which I did.

It still gives me pleasure to remember walking into my parents' bedroom for the first time ever, with a tray containing a teapot ,milk, sugar, two teacups and saucers, freshly made toast, butter and marmalade. I gently woke them up – in other words, I did not shout.

"Good morning, Mum. Good morning, Dad. I have brought you breakfast in bed," I said (not a big deal really as they had a teasmaid which not only woke them up of a morning with a cup of tea, but it also turned on the radio.).

"Oh, thank you," came the sleepy reply as they both regained consciousness, after a good night's sleep. They sat up in bed and I proudly placed the tray on my Mum's lap, and before they could say anything, I was gone. I then delivered two cups of tea to my brothers, however, they did not warrant the toast and marmalade. I was not going to miss them that much!

"Good morning, Mark and Rob," I warbled. "OK!" I shouted. "I have brought you a lovely cuppa!"

"Clear off!" replied my elder brother. Well that was the gist of what he said (you will appreciate that the first chapter is not the place to start using bad language or even allowing for Artistic Licence!).

"Can I move into your room now?" was the first response from my younger brother.

"Not yet," I replied. "I'll tell you when," and with that I was gone.

Unfortunately, neither my parents nor my two brothers appreciated my efforts, probably because it was only a quarter to six in the morning! But they soon forgave me, especially my younger brother, who could not wait to inherit my bedroom and indecently moved all of his belongings out of the room he shared with my elder brother and into mine, all before breakfast. I thought this was a little premature as I still had not even left the house by then. Dead man's shoes came to mind; well that's not quite true, as this was an expression which I do not believe I had ever heard before.

I never did find out why I had a room to myself while my two brothers had to share a room. I think it had something to do with the fact that my parents worked in hotels which required them to work until at least eight thirty at night and it was therefore incumbent (that's a posh word for so early in the book!) upon my elder brother to look after my younger brother while they were at work and they thought it would be easier to keep an eye on the youngster if they shared a room. Come to think of it, he was also expected to look after me as well, so why weren't we all in the same room? They probably realised the potential for chaos we could have caused if we were all in the same room, it was bad enough us being together during the daytime.

I found out later, on my first leave to be precise, that my younger brother had started the redecoration of my vacated bedroom before that very lunchtime. He painted the whole of *my* room, black, including the ceiling, much to the obvious delight of my parents who tactfully suggested he toned the decoration down a little by wallpapering the main wall with a white paper which had some irregular, thin black, vertical lines on top. I do not think they had even thought of sixty-minute makeovers in those days, never mind interior designers. At least their modification allowed you to see what was in the room without having to turn the light on first.

The hour of my departure arrived and I remember packing all my worldly goods and chef's gear into the side panniers of my Lambretta. In the early 1960s they were a "must have" form of transport for those teenagers whose parents would not let them have a motorbike. I remember that scooter with fond memories; it was a bright opalescent orange and had a six-foot aerial at the rear, with a fake squirrel's tail attached to its top. I never did understand the purpose of this aerial as the bike did not have a radio and even if it did, who ever heard of anyone listening to music whilst riding a motorbike or scooter? After all, you would never hear anything, even if you were able to get any reception. Perhaps it was designed as a telephone aerial so one could plug in one's bright red, eight inch, Bakelite telephone, like the one we had at home; we were dead trendy in those days, you know, except there was nowhere on the bike to plug it into (Bluetooth was not even a word in those days never mind someone inventing it). Come to think of it, I doubt whether I would even have been able to hear the ring tone from beneath my crash helmet even if I had found some way of connecting a phone.

But I do remember that this bike was cheap to buy – very cheap; in fact, it was free. No, I did not steal it, my parents – more accurately, my mother – bought it for me in an attempt to bribe me to come home regularly when I was on leave. Despite all its short comings, I was actually quite fond of that bike and was sorry to see it go when I did eventually trade it in for a bubble car. We teenagers sure knew how to live in those days!

Once packed, my mother and two brothers came out onto the driveway this makes it sound as if we had a posh house with space upon which to drive a car, when actually, we never had a car, so it is probably more accurate to describe it as a front path – sorry for the confusion, to wave me a fond farewell; well, I was grown up now and could not do with any soppy goodbyes! I sped off down the road, leaving behind the council owned semi-detached house we had lived in for the previous nine years. I must admit, I did not dare to look back, not because I could have crashed, but the emotion of the moment could easily have started me off, which of course would not have been cool, and so began my first solo journey to Southampton. My father had long since gone to work, he had left almost an hour earlier than necessary, courtesy of this morning's very early and rude awakening.

That journey was uneventful and I covered the ninety odd miles in just over two hours, the roads were much quieter back then and despite the fact that there were no speed cameras around, there were far more policemen on the beat and many more squad cars patrolling the roads, so it was unwise to exceed the speed limit. Or more importantly, not to get caught; remember, you do not get into trouble for doing wrong, you get into trouble for getting caught! When I reached the outskirts of Southampton, I managed to get myself hopelessly lost. Luckily, I was quickly able to find a policeman (unlike today) and duly stopped to ask him for directions.

You can imagine my horror when he ignored my request for directions and told me to empty my panniers and show him what I was carrying; you can imagine his response upon discovering my set of chef's knives, despite the fact that they were tightly rolled up in a canvas wallet. Things then went from bad to worse, as he informed me that two of my knives were illegal, as their blades were longer than the law allowed to be carried in the street. This immediately sent shivers down my spine as I imagined he was about to arrest me and march me off to jail, thereby preventing me from joining my ship.

Fortunately, he accepted my explanation when I showed him my brand new seaman's log book and my orders to report to the ship and so he allowed me to continue on my way, having given me the correct directions to follow.

At last I arrived safely at the allotted dock for the Queen Mary, only to find it empty. Panic set in. Where was the ship? Had I somehow missed it? Was this the right day? Was this the right time? Was I in the right place? Where should I go? Where would I sleep that night? All kinds of questions flashed through my mind. Thankfully, the guard on the gate allayed my fears when he explained that it was not yet high tide and so the ship had to weigh anchor off the Isle of Wight until the channel was deep enough for the ship to navigate up the Solent to its berth, a situation which was to repeat itself on many occasions during the next few years. This resulted in long waits for the tide to turn and allow us to dock and get ashore, a situation which was most frustrating, especially when you were due to go on leave once the ship eventually did dock.

The guard went on to explain that the ship was due within the hour and sure enough, some fifty minutes later, she finally came into view. I will always remember my first sight of this magnificent ship as she glided majestically into view, flanked by four sea going tugs, which gently pushed and nudged the 81,000-tonne (unladen) ship along the River Solent and into her home berth; what a magnificent sight, those three trademark red and black funnels rising elegantly above her gleaming white decks. It remains a wonder of modern seamanship to see such a large vessel being so smoothly manoeuvred into place without detracting from the natural grace this grand old lady of the sea undoubtedly possessed.

Then all of a sudden this magnificent spectacle was all over; there she sat, docked alongside with her gangplanks lowered and her human cargo spewing out from her various levels onto the waiting Pullman train, which would whisk them off to London without further ado. It was now my turn and I gingerly made my way up the crew gangplank for the first time, taking great care not to topple over into the sea, which was rather stupid really as there were rope railings on either side and it was almost impossible to fall in. Before I knew it, I had entered the bowels of this huge ship, and it made me realize just how Jonah must have felt as he was swallowed into the mouth of the whale; at least I did know that I would be coming out again though.

At the top of the gangplank, I was met by the ship's Master at Arms (the equivalent of an on board Police Chief – a man not to be messed with), who, after the necessary security checks, organised my safe passage to the Head Chef's Office. By this time my stomach was churning like a concrete mixer, as my nerves took over and I was eternally grateful that the formalities were very short and I was extremely thankful to be quickly shown to my cabin by my new roommate, Alistair, a young Scot from Edinburgh. Upon reaching the safety of my room, I had the embarrassment of suffering my first ever bout of seasickness, which was to last all of the three days we were tied up alongside in port. A most inauspicious start to my "naval career".

On the morning of the third day, I had recovered sufficiently enough to venture up into the galley; you can imagine my embarrassment, seasick for three days, while the ship was tied up alongside, in her berth! Most embarrassing. Luckily, this was not an unusual phenomenon, and many a new recruit had shared my indignity and I was later to learn that seasickness is often psychosomatic – the result of the mind ruling the body.

Indeed, I have never been seasick since that time, not even when the ship was being tossed around like a cork by forty foot waves during subsequent winter storms. Consequently, I was not made to feel any more foolish than I already felt and I was allowed to commence my kitchen duties without further ado.

For the first time, I realised just how big the ship actually was, as there were five galleys besides the one for the crew. The Veranda Grill was right at the top of the ship, above the bridge, and was only open for dinner. It was for the exclusive use of the first-class passengers and even they had to pay a supplement to eat in such a superior a la Carte Restaurant, which could only accommodate a maximum of forty covers. There was no menu and passengers were required to pre-book prior to ten o'clock that morning and they also had to identify their menu for dinner. They literally could order whatever they wished, as long as the ingredients were readily available on board the ship. Everything was then freshly cooked to order and served in the most lavish of styles.

There was even a one hundred pound reward for anyone ordering a dish which could not be produced because no one knew what it was (mind you, the staff were supported by the largest and most up to date culinary library ever assembled) and as a consequence, this prize had only been claimed once since the Second World War. This was because the staff who manned this kitchen were both the cream of the Cunard Line and also widely considered to be among the best chefs in the catering industry at that time.

The second restaurant was the first-class salon, which catered for all those passengers who relished all the finer things in life, during an age of elegance and glamour where dressing for dinner was a pleasure rather than a chore. The whole experience was universally regarded as one of the best in the world, and featured the exemplary service for which Cunard is still famed. The first-class dining room with its original and lavish murals (including a feature of a crystal model of the ship which would sail backwards and forwards across a map of the Atlantic to pinpoint the exact position of the ship for the passengers, solid Italian granite pillars, original wood block flooring, solid silver cutlery and serving dishes, which were used both for silver service and Guerdon service where the meal is finished off from heated lamps on trolleys and flambé work, all served onto genuine bone china), proved to be a wonderland of grace and opulence. Each evening the atmosphere was further enhanced by a live dance band which provided discrete background music in the early evening, progressing onto music to dance to as the evening progressed. Dinner really was a social event, made all the more exiting by the surroundings and the supreme excellence of the staff.

The list of celebrities who regularly travelled on the Queen Mary was endless and included such well-known personalities as Sir Winston Churchill; Elizabeth Taylor and Richard Burton; Marlene Deitrich; Bing Crosby; Sir John Mills (who was infamous for his power walks around the deck each morning); David Niven; Fred Astaire (who, surprise, surprise, used to dance the night away with the most glamorous of passengers aboard) and Cary Grant (who christened the Mary "the eighth wonder of the world") and so the list went on.

The third restaurant was the cabin class, which provided for passengers who aspired to a greater level of luxury and comfort than was available in the tourist class, but could not afford to pay the price for the full luxury of the first class; the standard here equated to those found in the equivalent of a good four star hotel. These passengers received a similar choice of food, but did not have quite the grandiose of surroundings and service extras which were enjoyed by the first-class passengers. Also, the music was provided by a trio of musicians rather than a full dance band.

Tourist class (or steerage, as it was once known), was the cheapest way to travel but it still offered a standard of service which equated to a three star hotel, providing a wide range of good wholesome cuisine with four or five choices on each course of the meal, all silver serviced, naturally.

Finally, there was the Kosher Galley, which met the religious needs of the many Jewish passengers, who were the main users of the ship's luxurious suites and therefore made economic sense to cater specifically for their needs The kitchen staff, the specially killed meat and the kosher food were all blessed by a Rabbi prior to sailing as it was impractical to carry a Rabbi on all sailings solely to effect a blessing prior to each meal.
In
eed, there must have been sailings when this facility was not required or used. Naturally the range of menus, the quality of dishes and service were all of the highest standard.

Despite my poor start, my first work day proved to be my lucky day as I was assigned to the larder section of the kitchen (the area responsible for all hors d'oeuvres, salads, cold buffets, cold sauces, ice carvings, pre-dinner canapés and cold cooked garniture, as required by the main areas of the kitchen). It was my good fortune, because no actual cooking is done in this area and consequently it never gets hot, like every other area of the kitchen. Also, the larder was situated on the outside of the ship and so it was possible to have the port holes open during the more clement weather, which provided us with fresh air rather than the air recycled by the air conditioning unit operating in the rest of the kitchen.

My immediate workmates proved to be a wonderful group of people, each with their own individual traits which helped to make life on board so worthwhile. The boss, or larder chef was Johnie, a married man who came from Southampton. He was quite a tall man with a very portly figure; I would even go so far as to say he was fat (as long as he never heard me as he thought he was a fine figure of a man!), his face was extremely rugged and his features were very sharp and angular as if his face had been hewn from a block of granite. His hairstyle would have been more in fashion during World War II as he was one of the original "Brylcream Boys". He had a small tattoo of a crown and anchor on the back of each wrist, which he admitted he had done one day when he was both drunk and bored in New York when he was only nineteen years of age. You could always hear him coming as the only footwear he ever wore were sabots, which made a hell of a racket when the solid wood clomped upon the tiled, steel floors.

Johnnie was a lifelong sailor who had joined the Queen Mary straight from school and had worked all his life on this one ship. During this period, he had worked his way up through the ranks to become one of the senior staff in the kitchen and despite his rank, he had a reputation as a practical joker and loved nothing better than to think of new initiations for rookie crewmen who were joining the ship for the first time. My induction was quite simple and supposedly harmless; he asked me if I liked to go to dances as the Captain welcomed all new staff, especially if it was their first trip to sea, to his sailing night ball. Naturally, I thought that it would be rather nice to meet the Captain and be welcomed on board personally, so I indicated that I would like to attend, only to be told that he had forwarded the tickets to the pastry chef. So off I went to the pastry section, only to be told that he had sent the tickets onto the butcher, so off I went, he sent me on to the printer, and so it went on, with me being passed from one area of the ship to another.

An hour and a half later, I found myself at the door of the Staff Captain's office, and after a brief wait, I was ushered in to explain my presence. Imagine my confusion when he told me to either return to work or swim back to Southampton! (or words which amounted to these sentiments). I asked him if he knew how to get back to the kitchens and he told me where to go! So I returned to

Johnnie for an explanation. He could not believe that I had the perseverance to pursue this all the way up to the Staff Captain and then had the nerve to invade the inner sanctum of the "god".

This is where I got my naval nickname "Percy", short for perseverance. Yes, I had to explain this whole saga every time someone asked where I got my nickname. Nevertheless, this process of being sent from one section of the ship to another, helped me to find my way around the ship far quicker than if I had been left to my own devices, especially as each of my tormentors were kind enough to provide directions onto my next antagonist.

I must admit that I preferred my induction to some of the later ones I witnessed, especially the one where a fairly obnoxious young man known as "sinex" (because of his ability to get right up people's noses), had a rope tied around his chest and under his armpits before being lowered down the "chute", the metal tube that went from the kitchen down into the sea, which was used to dispose of degradable rubbish. Unfortunately, a larger than normal wave hit the side of the ship at the same time as he arrived at the bottom of this tube and instead of just having his feet dipped into the Atlantic, he was completely submerged! Luckily, he suffered no long-term ill effects but he did calm down a lot after this experience.

There were two permanent assistant cooks working with Johnnie; Scouser, a twenty-two-year old loner from Liverpool, who liked nothing better than to keep fit and was the original "my body is a temple" man. He very seldom socialised with the rest of us, not even for a beer and remained a total enigma all the time I was at sea.

Then there was Lenny, the only person I have ever met who actually admitted to coming from the Isle of Wight, not that I have anything against the Isle of Wight, just it is a place everyone goes to, not the place people come from, if you know what I mean. It was where he had been married and he had a small house only yards away from the ferry terminal. Here was your Mr Average. He never did anything to attract attention, he just kept his head down and did his job without any fuss; indeed, he was the kind of person you could pass in the street without even noticing him. The only significant personal fact I ever found out about him was that he was saving all his money to buy a pub in Shanklin and he would then give up the life at sea as soon as possible.

The second in command of the larder who was technically known as the Chef Hors d'Oeuvrier, who was to become my boss, was Kenny. He was in his early fifties and had one glass eye (he lost his original eye during the War). He was an alcoholic, which resulted in him having the shakes so badly each morning that when he held a knife, he could chop parsley without intentionally moving his hand! To overcome Cunard's "no spirits in the kitchen" rule, Kenny always filled his tea mug from a quart lemonade bottle, which he kept on his workbench, and, which he kept full of vodka and tonic! Because of their similar appearance, no one ever suspected the truth. He was quite a short man and his face was a reflection of his apparently hard life being extremely craggy; he seemed to have almost as many facial contours as a bulldog, plus a wart on his left cheek, which always seemed to attract your attention. His thinning hair was a light ginger in colour and he wore it in a style which Bobby Charlton was to make famous some years later (thin strands combed over his naked skull).

Despite all his personal problems, Kenny was one of the most knowledgeable and artistic chefs I have ever met and to see him carve a two foot square block of solid ice into a beautiful swan, using only a small saw, hammer and chisel, blow lamp and salt, was truly remarkable (although he hated this aspect of his work, as he could not stand being cold, and to do ice carvings one had to work in the deep freeze for a couple of hours). Kenny's main passion (besides the drink) was vintage cars and as soon as we docked, be it Southampton or New York, he would be down the gang plank and climb into a superb vintage car which he owned and had garaged in each country. He would not be seen again until he was next due for work. I never did fathom out how he was able to drive these cars without ever having an accident, given the amount of alcohol which must have been ever present in his bloodstream. Probably because there were far fewer vehicles on the roads, and these cars were nowhere near as fast, plus there were far fewer accidents on the road.

The final permanent member of our team was a guy whom I am certain modelled for the logo of a famous motorway restaurant chain, being as round as he was tall. He went under the name of Mickey Rooney (which was actually his real name), not only because of a similar facial resemblance to the famous film star, but also because he had apparently been married seven times. This he claimed was the reason he was at sea; here was the only place he could earn enough money to pay all his alimony, and, it also prevented him from remarrying so often! Not to mention the fact that he could not accidentally bump into any of his mother-in-laws while at sea.

Mickey was the comedian of the team and never appeared (on the surface) to take anything seriously, spending all his waking hours wise cracking, which could be a little tedious at times. But as he was such a likeable character, nobody ever told him to shut up or took offence at his repartee. His other annoying trait was the fact that he was a pipe smoker, and so when he sneaked off for a crafty smoke, he was gone for half an hour at a time! It took at least this length of time to clean, fill, light and smoke a pipe of tobacco. He was a close friend of Kenny and they spent much of their free time together; watching Mickey prise himself in and out of Kenny's cars was a favourite pastime of most of the crew on docking days and the aft deck was often crowded just to witness Mickey achieve the near impossible feat of shoehorning his body into the front passenger seat of the car (if only we had had a cine camera in those days!).

Finally, there were the three kitchen porters who made up our team. Each sailing, we were allocated different people because of the boring nature of their work either in the plonge (wash up area), peeling potatoes (an eighteen-hour-a-day operation) or supporting areas like ours where they did the washing up (of both dishes and salad ingredients; collecting our provisions from the lower decks.

The other important duty was to collect our beer as it was a very long day and the bar was quite a way from the kitchen. It appears working with us was a very popular job, not only was it a cool area to work in, but also, we were considered to be the nicest team to work with, as we were not temperamental.

One porter told me we were the only team on the whole ship that helped with the morning scrub down in readiness for the officer of the day's inspection, which took place at eleven thirty each morning. (This involved clearing all surfaces of all food etc. and scrubbing down the whole room, from floor to ceiling, with a hot soapy water power hose before rinsing off and drying.) He did not realize the only reason we helped him was to shorten the wipe down process so that we could continue with our work and thereby avoiding putting ourselves under pressure to be ready for the lunch service time!

Four days after leaving Southampton we passed the bell tower which signified we had entered the Hudson River and were about to welcome the pilot and tugs, which would take us safely into Pier 90 and our docking station.

Here was another experience of a lifetime and my first view of the New York skyline. This is one of the modern Seven Wonders of the World. The sight of this city's skyline gracefully sliding past, is something which can only be experienced and cannot be described in a way which will do it justice. This was an opinion which never changed in the thirty-two trips I subsequently made to the Big Apple, though I never did discover how it got this nickname?

CHAPTER TWO

The Queen Mary carried almost twelve hundred crew members when fully staffed; this included the deck hands, engineers and the staff working in the following areas; catering and bars; butchers; fishmongers; grocers; printers; hair and beauty; domestics, including the bursars, housekeepers and laundry staff, and entertainment staff.

Each area of work had their living quarters in a different part of the ship and on different decks, for example, the chefs, waiters and bar staff occupied the stern of the ship on the decks just above and on the waterline. Engineering staff lived in the bow of the ship; the other ranks lived amidships, and most cabins were situated on the deck adjacent to the sea or just below the waterline.

Naturally, it goes without saying that the higher one's rank, the better the accommodation you were entitled to; we student cooks shared a substantial cabin large enough for three or four people to live in comfortably. We each had our own wardrobe, complete with its own chest of drawers, both of which were lockable to protect our privacy and the security of our most valued possessions. There was a small sink and a mirror for washing and cleaning of teeth etc. We slept in bunk beds, each of which had its own thick curtain to provide both privacy and darkness, which was essential because of our staggered sleeping patterns. At the time, this was considered to be quite luxurious and provided us with quite a privileged existence.

On the other hand, the waiters were less privileged as they were domiciled in large dormitory like cabins, which housed between eight and twelve people, all the same sex

– male naturally. (I still do not understand why there were no waitresses aboard any of the liners at that time – probably due to the complications of accommodation). They all slept in bunk beds, which were separated only by a pair of lockers, providing one full lengthlocker per person. Each bunk had its own set of curtains; I used to think that these cabins were extremely overcrowded, totally lacking in privacy as they did not even have a wash hand basin in their room, so the occupants had to leave their cabin and walk down the corridor to the communal shower room, just to get a wash or brush their teeth.

Senior kitchen and restaurant ratings either shared their cabin with one another or had their own cabin, depending on their seniority, each complete with full length wardrobes, a separate chest of drawers and their own sink unit! Now that was the height of luxury. I never did discover what accommodation the female staff who worked in housekeeping, laundry and the bursars office had, and come to think of it, I never even knew where their cabins were situated.

Each section of cabins had what was known as a "Glory Hole Steward", who was solely employed to look after the working crew members. Their duties included making their bunks, changing their sheets and linen, cleaning the floors and corridors, cleaning the communal showers and toilets, organizing personal washing, and to generally keep the cabins tidy and to prevent the whole area from becoming an absolute slum (bearing in mind that the whole ship was subjected to a meticulous daily inspection by the officer of the day). Also, each steward was an absolute necessity because of the irregular and extremely long hours worked by everyone, once at sea. We chefs, for example, normally started work, or "turned to" (started work) at 0700 hours each morning and we worked through until 1500 hours, with a staggered ninety-minute break sometime during the morning. This break was scheduled at either at 1030 or 1200hrs and nearly everyone used this time to catch up on their sleep.

After luncheon service had finished, normally around 1500 hours, there was a two-hour break until 1700 hours, except that is for the skeleton crew, whose morning break was taken between 1200 hours and 1330 hours. They worked on until 1700 hours before they had their two-hour break, returning to duty in time for the evening dinner service. The whole team then worked through until the completion of this meal, normally around 2300 hours, bearing in mind that the clocks went back an hour at midnight, on our westward trip towards New York and then they were turned forward an hour, at midnight, on our return journey to Southampton.

Consequently, it goes without saying that we had very little time to look after our cabins ourselves, even if we wanted to. Naturally, there was an expectation to enhance the pay of our steward, as this was one of the poorest paid jobs on board the ship which no one objected to as these people were all absolutely indispensable and worth their weight in gold. Our steward was a matchstick of a Welshman, who stood less than five foot six inches tall, when fully erect and weighed less than ten stone when fully dressed and wearing his overcoat. He had thin brown hair, which he always wore extremely long and down to his collar; his ears were pointed and seemed to protrude further than usual. He claimed that he had trained them this way as it was essential to keep his glasses on; furthermore, he had the biggest set of buck teeth I have ever known and they were all his own! Indeed, he was actually proud of these teeth and would often make jokes about us less fortunate people. His name was Rabbett – guess what his nickname was? No, don't be silly, it was not Welsh Rabbit! It was Bunny – I bet you would never have guessed that in a month of Sundays! He was an incredible guy who never seemed to sleep, as he was always available whenever you needed something. Bunny was an extremely well-organised guy and did a fabulous job in keeping our living area immaculate, which made us the envy of every other area of the ship as their stewards were not always so conscientious and did not necessarily do such a good job.

However, Bunny was no saint and he liked nothing better than to go ashore and spend a couple of hours drinking in the bar, which was predominately used by the crew from Cunard ships, opposite to Pier 90. Once he had had his fill, he would go into one of the other dockside bars frequented by the crews from other shipping companies. As you can imagine, it was not long before he antagonised others and a fight would break out, with Bunny inevitably at the centre of any and all disturbances. What was remarkable was the fact that he never seemed to get seriously hurt in any of these contretemps, he just loved to fight!

In those days, the most common method of dealing with this sort of trouble was for the bar staff to phone the police, before attempting to ease the combatants out of the door and onto the dockside. The police would then surround the fighters and move in with their night sticks. Apparently, if the police arrested anyone, they would have to do all the paperwork involved and then they would have to attend any court proceedings, in their own time. Whereas, by using the nightsticks, it meant that when the brawlers recovered consciousness, none of them ever wanted to continue fighting.

Bunny, like everyone else, had his own "nice little earner", which was to organise a sweepstake for his "boys" (as he called us) each trip, which, for a dollar going out or a pound coming back, you could buy a ticket, which in reality was one minute of the hour, and the winner was the person who purchased the precise minute of arrival, as announced by the Captain. This was the precise time when the ship officially passed the Bell Tower at the mouth of the harbour in New York or the Nab Tower in Southampton waters, a most useful way of earning $30 (approximately two weeks' wages for a student cook), and if you were the lucky winner or $10 if you were either side of the winning number, leaving $10 dollars for Bunny. I actually won twice.

At this point, I should explain the typical "economy "of any passenger ship during this period of the early sixties, was to ensure that everyone shared in all "unearned income". This particularly benefited those members of the crew who were not in a position to directly earn this extra money themselves. There were the fortunate staff who received tips directly from the passengers, which included the waiters, bar staff, stewards etc. So they, in turn, would be "charged" by the other members of staff, who had a service to sell, which, in most cases, were those nice little extras which made life at sea less boring and more bearable. The following "extras" were the most common practices:

- The crew members who received tips from passengers, would pay a "service surcharge" to a section or team of the kitchen staff to provide them with food/meals for the duration of that trip, as this was far more preferable to eating in the crew galley, which was extremely basic food and apparently, and not cooked to a very high quality. This agreement allowed that crew member to choose any dish from the first-class passenger menus or even have access to the specially made dishes produced unofficially in the kitchen for crew members as "a treat " to break the monotony and repetitiveness of the dishes found on the normal menus; yes, you can actually and often did get fed up with an overabundance of prime steaks and caviar! Indeed it was not unusual for crew members to actually crave the simpler foods like corned beef sandwiches, which most of the crew grew up on during and after the Second World War and were so popular that these sandwiches became a very lucrative sideline, so much so, that it was possible to charge member of the crew a further supplement for such a luxury; it was so profitable that Johnnie (the larder chef) used to buy ten-pound tins of corned beef in a New York meat wholesaler, specifically to satisfy this demand! Normally the ship carried such vast supplies of products that minor pilferage went unnoticed, but in this particular case, the stock level carried on board was so small, we only carried three ten-pound tins per trip. which were all essential for the corned beef hash cakes which appeared upon the menu. Consequently, there literally was never any to spare, hence the need to buy in these extra supplies.

- Waiters, eager to increase their tips and income, would pay the printers for complete "virgin" presentation packs of menus used on that trip. The waiters would in turn "sell" them onto their passengers as high quality souvenirs, whilst at the same time emphasising to the customer how rare and difficult it was to get hold of such pristine sets. Naturally, this was an extremely informal transaction because the waiters never produced bills or receipts and so this said income was never declared nor taxable! It was further rumoured that the waiters had a second sideline when they "accessed" (nudge, nudge, wink, wink!) souvenir sets of china and cutlery, which consisted of any item which had either the logo or a picture of the ship embossed upon them. These items were obtained from the china and silver locker room staff, either to replace breakages or for money, naturally. The waiters were then able to recycle these goods to the passengers for a mutually acceptable financial reward, fixed by the waiter of course. As you might expect, the natural china breakages were substantial, particularly during rough seas, and so these "losses" did not attract too much attention and the cutlery had a habit of falling down the chute into the sea together with the real degradable waste; well, it saved on washing up! It has to be said that these "souvenir sets" consisted merely of a cup and saucer or a knife and fork or similar; these sets were never whole place settings or services as these would attract too much attention and were too bulky to fit in passengers luggage, also, the "stock "required for such ventures would have been phenomenal bearing in mind each trip could have a couple of thousand passengers on board. Other popular souvenirs were apparently available through the cabin stewardesses and included sheets, pillow cases and towels of various sizes – sounds familiar even today? Come to think of it, I wish I had acquired some of these souvenirs, they are worth a small fortune according to the TV auction programs, so who am I to argue?

- The butchers and greengrocers "bunce" was to sell apple boxes (which they had filled with quality raw food "left over" from that trip) to any interested members of the crew for only one pound sterling. These sales took place each time the ship was about to dock in our home port of Southampton. This transaction even included an "official receipt", which replicated genuine receipts obtained from a store in New York and was accurate down to the shop's header and a date which coincided with our being in the Big Apple (this was produced on board by the printer's) to prove the enclosed foods were purchased in New York. These boxes would typically contain a selection of meats, including prime steaks, chops of all types, chickens and at least one whole joint, which was large enough to feed a substantial family. They were then filled up with the more unusual fruits and vegetables, all of which, were extremely popular and in great demand with married crewmen and members of the crew who were going home on a two-week leave. A few years later, there was a major scandal which resulted in all the activities of the butchers, printers and greengrocers being investigated by the police. This resulted in legal prosecutions and prison sentences of up to eight years each on charges of theft and deception.

- In the Dining room, when a waiter required quicker service from the "trancheur" (the chef who carved a large joint of meat in front of the customer from a heated trolley), they were expected to "encourage" him with a small remuneration for a prompt service, safe in the knowledge that such efficiency would please their customers and therefore enhance the tip they could expect at the end of the trip.

- Every time the crew went ashore, they required a baggage docket for each piece of luggage they took with them, and guess what...? If you wanted a docket for more than the regulation one item, for example your apple box full of goodies, you had to "purchase" the extra docket from the kitchen clerk, who was responsible for issuing these documents to all catering, bar and domestic staff. This was his little sideline.

- Because of the pressure of work, one seldom had time to do the menial things like washing and ironing your clothes (bearing in mind that all uniforms were supplied and laundered by the ship), so guess what? You paid someone else to do it, which necessitated a payment naturally, but it was worth every penny, especially when you saw the conditions the laundry staff worked under down in the bowels of the ship. Also, it was often up to ten weeks before some people went on leave and returned home to mummy or their wife; consequently, things began to smell a bit, if you had saved up all your washing!

From these examples, it becomes apparent as to how the "economy" of the ship ensured that all the monies generated, were equally redistributed amongst the crew members who contributed or supported the people receiving this wealth. Most of the tips were given on docking days and it is not surprising to learn that this redistribution happened on the same day – once every five days when the ship docked.

Another popular way of generating money, when staff found themselves to be financially embarrassed in New York, was to make a visit to the local blood bank, where one could sell a pint of blood for between twenty to sixty dollars, depending on the rarity of your blood grouping. Therefore, if you were anything other than a blood group "O", you were a potential walking gold mine. After you had given your "armful" of blood, the hospital even gave you a cup of tea and a chocolate biscuit, as part of the deal! The down side of this was, the nurse recommended that you used your money to purchase a slap up meal to speed up the regeneration of the donated blood ,although most of us went for a burger, took in a movie, then spent the rest of the evening in a bar and still had change!

Although it has to be said, that if you walked outside and got hit by a car and needed your own blood back, it would have cost you five times as much as the blood bank had just paid you!

When the crew members originally signed on to the ship – even after a leave – you signed what was known as an allotment, which meant that you agreed to have either a percentage of or all of your basic salary paid directly into your bank; this was designed to prevent staff from either drinking away their salary or losing it all at cards or merely frittering it away. It also ensured that their families had access to some money while the crew member was away. The vast majority of crew members signed over all their salary to the bank and then lived purely on of their overtime, which they could draw upon each docking day, or they would simply rely upon their share of the money from the "redistribution", which I explained previously.

Overtime was an interesting phenomena, as it was not physically possible to work any hours longer than we already did, it was only possible to work harder when the ship was busier. Therefore, there was a standing agreement whereby all hours worked at sea, after midday on a Saturday, were paid at time and a half the standard rate of pay. Also, all day Sunday at sea, was paid at double time. On top of this, there was a daily overtime sliding scale, which was calculated according to the total number of passengers on board, with a minimum of three hours per day for the first five hundred passengers, then another hour for every hundred passengers thereafter. This was on top of the enhanced rate for Saturday and Sunday – lovely jubbly. All of which meant, that it was not unusual for the gross monthly salary to become the amount we were paid each week – and we still managed to build up a healthy bank balance.

As a result of this level of income, coupled with the fact that we received full board and lodgings and our uniforms were both provided and laundered (all tax free at that time), meant we had a minimum of outgoings to worry about, and consequently, most members of the crew were able to pursue an expensive "hobby". Kenny had his vintage cars; Mickey was saving up to buy his own Public House (he could then cut out the middle man by being attached intravenously to the beer supply, without having to waste time drinking it); John was investing his money in property, which he then rented out to students at Southampton University; several others were saving up to purchase their own catering businesses, of one sort or another, but the more discerning of us youngsters invested our money more sensibly. For example, nearly every time we arrived in New York, we would go to the airport (there was only one in the city in those days) and fly off somewhere, as believe it or not, we had become bored with New York (just as long as this trip allowed us a couple of hours in that destination and ensured that we could get back to the ship in time for our next shift, we did not worry over much about our destination). This was the era of the consumer society and we certainly were eager participants.

Accordingly, we student cooks would spend most of our off-duty time on the outward trip to New York scrutinising the timetables of the different American airlines, looking for trips which fulfilled our simple requirements. Sometimes we had to spend the night in a hotel room, as it was not possible to fly out and back in the same day; remember that in America, you pay for the room and not per person using the room, irrespective of how many people occupied that room. As you can imagine, our room was often like the Black Hole of Calcutta and the smell was overpowering, and I do not just mean from smelly feet!

During these trips, we spent most of our time away in a convenient local bar or diner anyway. Occasionally, we even treated ourselves and went to the movies. Irrespective, we thought that this was money well spent, especially as we always felt we had had a marvelous time, that was of course, if we could remember anything about the trip. The other advantage of having a good level of disposable income was, we were able to shop either in America or in the UK, which gave us access to all the latest gear and trappings for our cabins, including all the latest records (which were still on vinyl in those days) and tapes (they were the fore runner to CDs) not to mention the most up-to-date clothes one could ever wish for. All of which was fine as long as one never took those items purchased in America, ashore in England, because as soon as that happened you were liable to pay duty on these items, although technically duty was payable once items were brought into territorial waters, which was difficult to enforce. However, if you got caught trying to evade paying duty or smuggling, the customs officers were entitled to search your cabin for other items upon which duty had not been paid. Under such circumstances, you were fined, charged the unpaid duty on everything found and even had all these goods confiscated as well... an expensive business and one very few crew members ever risked. Even though they could afford the fines etc. most crew members simply paid the duty up front rather than risk losing their jobs, which was often the result of being caught smuggling.

One of the favorite covert ways the English customs officers had of catching these smugglers, was to simply mingle with the crew when they caught the train to London and then join the inevitable card school which started during the journey (obviously they were in civvies and not their custom uniforms). These guys and gals always appeared to be excellent card players and they nearly always won, which in turn encouraged the crew members who were losing, to offer their illegal contraband in lieu of further gambling stakes, either by trying to sell these items to anyone interested or, if acceptable, by using it as the ante on further games. Once off of the train, in the London railway terminal, the customs officers arrested the targeted crew members for smuggling; strangely enough, the covert officers always appeared to keep their winnings or underwrite their losses (though I am given to understand this very rarely happened).

Another lucrative and legal practice, which most crew members indulged in, was to take full advantage of the fact that they were allowed to have 40 cigarettes on them each time they left the ship and went ashore; the allowance only increased to 200 cigarettes when you went on leave, and so it was common practice to return to the ship five or six times a day to collect further supplies. While the crew members often appeared like squirrels looking for or hiding their nuts, by running backward and forward to the ship to collect their 40 Capstan or Senior Service cigarettes. Once ashore, the cigarettes were normally left in the safe keeping of a reliable friend who had usually been parked in a convenient pub.

This supply of cigarettes, once safely gathered, would then be posted home in bulk, in readiness for their next home leave. In this way, the crew members accumulated quite a cache, even the non-smokers would join in as they could sell their cigarettes to friends or relatives; still, it was not unusual for smokers to amass far more than they needed and they too would sell their surplus, thereby underwriting their whole leave! Naturally, postage costs were substantially cheaper and the service was much more reliable in those days than is currently the case. I never understood why all local post offices did not have to X-ray all small packages near ports, as they could easily have earned the government a small fortune from the tax avoidance!

This practice was quite often extended to bottles of spirits as well, except they were more carefully packaged for posting naturally, with protective layers of bubble wrap before being placed inside padded postage envelopes which were marked fragile, prior to posting. Alcohol was a much more lucrative commodity than cigarettes because a bottle of spirits could be purchased for the equivalent of less than 25p per litre bottle while at sea, which represented less than a quarter of the price paid in the shops on shore! Also, having a stock of booze waiting at home for your next leave, ensured we always had tremendous parties once we did go home on leave. Furthermore, there was always a surplus of bottles to sell (at a substantial profit of course), which in turn, meant that we generated enough extra income to make our leave less boring, bearing in mind all our friends were working during the day time.

To be fair the summer was a good time in Eastbourne, as every summer it was invaded by thousands of foreign students wishing to learn English and two thirds of these were young, nubile females – mainly from Scandinavia – who spent every afternoon after their language classes on the beach in their bikinis trying to get their bodies tanned; best of all they were usually alone, as in no male companions! All of which more than fulfilled the wildest dreams of every young hot blooded male teenager who was lucky enough to witness such a bevy of gorgeous blond beauties. Best of all, being on the beach it did not cost us anything apart from the occasional ice cream!

In the evening, these same young ladies could be found in the local coffee bars; drinking in pubs was not the vogue for teenagers way back then, although it was common practice to adjourn to someone's flat later in the evening for a party which certainly did have alcohol. I was always amazed by the way in which the alcohol seemed to appear out of someone's pocket or handbag and every time there seemed to be more than sufficient booze to last until the early hours of the following morning. Come to think of it, the girls continuously surprised me by completing their English course successfully, taking into consideration the combination of the late night parties and their early morning classes. But they did, which meant that their final parties were double celebrations, exam success coupled with a farewell party! Any excuse – not that we needed an excuse – we were young!

I presume that I do not have to explain the number of young ladies that had their hearts broken by these holiday romances and pending departures, not to mention the number of impossible promises of undying love, which were made. But that's what happened in the sixties, and still happens, because the students still roll into Eastbourne every summer and the vast majority still appear to be female!

CHAPTER THREE

The work of the hors d'oeuvres section, to which I was assigned, was to prepare all the cold starters on the menu; all pre-dinner canapés; all ice carvings; the carving of all meat found on the cold buffet at lunch time and the carving of the featured hot roasted joint from the heated trolley in the evening. On the surface of it, there did not appear to be very much work involved in this role and therefore, it is necessary expand upon this work, bearing in mind that there was only Kenny (the hors d'oeuvrier) an assistant cook, myself (a novice student cook) and the shared kitchen Porter to carry out all this work.

The simplest part of the starters were the three items which were served as individual dishes; these included items such as:

Oak smoked side of Scotch Salmon with Capers

Delice de Foie Gras a la Strasbourg

Chilled Seafood Cocktail

Beluga Caviar

The work involved in the preparation of the whole side of smoked salmon, was first to remove all the remaining bones by first of all removing all the rib bones in a sheet with a sharp filleting knife, and then removing the remaining backbones by plucking them out individually with a pair of pliers (which were kept specifically for this purpose). The fish was then shaped to remove the discoloration caused during the smoking process and to give a more uniform and acceptable appearance. Finally, the side of salmon was lightly brushed with olive oil to give a light sheen and prevent it from drying out, before being placed upon a marble slab, together with a dish of capers and finally, garnished with lettuce and a sculptured lemon.

The standard accompaniment of brown bread and butter was provided by the pantry section. The finished salmon was "shaved" by one of our team on the buffet in the restaurant; the head chef was adamant that if you could not read a newspaper through the salmon, it was cut too thick, and he often reprimanded us for failing to comply with this requirement (the real reason of course was, it exceeded his laid down portion, and affected his profit margin).

The Foie Gras – a genuine high quality liver pate commercially made from goose livers and truffles – was removed from its tubular tin, divided into four and then dressed onto four separate services of a silver flat with a salad garnish. The accompaniment of freshly made Melba Toast was obtained separately from the pantry section and the whole service was placed on the cold buffet above crushed ice, until collected by the waiter, it was then sliced and plated in the restaurant by the waiter, from their Guerdon trolley, in front of their customer.

Unfortunately, the waiters often "forgot" to return the silver flats to the buffet once they had finished serving their customers and their colleagues had to run around the restaurant like the original headless chickens, looking for the Foie Gras! Indeed, there were often "handbags at dawn" (many of the waiters were highly temperamental or effeminate and were easily moved to powder puff violence), usually on the aft deck after work, because of the arguments caused by this neglect!

The Seafood Cocktail varied each mealtime and the options included crab, lobster, prawns or mixed seafood etc. and they were dressed into silver coupes, on top of a bed of finely chopped lettuce (a chiffonade) and then they were dressed with a generous portion of Cumberland Sauce (homemade mayonnaise, tomato sauce and Worcester Sauce to me and you) and finally they were finished with cayenne pepper, chopped parsley and a wedge of lemon. (All dressings used in the larder, including the mayonnaise, were made fresh each day naturally.) The finished dishes were then sunk into a larger silver dish or timbale, full of crushed ice. They were served with brown bread and butter obtained separately from the pantry section by the waiter.

Caviar comes from the roe of the sturgeon and no two roes can ever be mixed because of the subtle black color differences between any two fish, similar in many ways, to the color differences between two different batches of paint applied on the same wall.

Therefore, each roe is used firstly to fill one pound tins; if there is sufficient left over, it is then used to fill half pound tins, and finally the remainder is used to fill one and two ounce pots. (I know we have gone metric since then and the current units are sold in kilograms and grams!)

Caviar was and still is a very expensive commodity and the ship used the one pound pots which were placed onto the back of the ice carving (swans were the most popular), surrounded by the garniture of sieved hard-boiled egg whites, chopped onions and sieved egg yolks, plus blinis naturally (a dropped Russian pancake). The caviar and the swan were "towed" on a trolley to the customer's table and served by the waiter, using a special caviar spoon, which is similar to a silver teaspoon. I remember one lady who was trying to make an impression by flamboyantly ordering the caviar and demanded a "proper portion," only to reject it once she tasted it, because she said it must have been off as it tasted extremely salty and slightly fishy!

Because of its high price, it was not usual to include it in the "menus" offered to crew members; however, if someone particularly asked for caviar (and were prepared to pay the going rate for it), the shortfall in the tin could always be made up by adding a little high quality oil to the remaining caviar, which caused the eggs to swell up slightly and hide any resulting shortfall.

All the above dishes could be obtained in individual dishes from the larder if required, usually because the demand for the services in the restaurant was so high that customers had an unacceptable wait and this alternative relieved the pressure on the waiters for a slick service, which of course, influenced the size of their tips, but more importantly kept everyone happy – waiters, managers and passengers.

The mixed hors d'oeuvres, once made, were dressed upon six trolleys; each had twelve raviers (oblong china dishes), which fitted into silver frames, which could be then rotated manually, allowing the customers to see all the options safely without tipping their contents all over the floor. This revolving trolley also facilitated the silver service of the selected items.

Examples of these selections included:

Brislings in oil
(A small fish of the sprat family, fished in the North Sea, eighteen to twenty-four per tin)

Eggs Remoulade
(Sliced hard boiled eggs, on a bed of salad and coated with a Remoulade Sauce)

Antipasto Italienne

(Turned mixed vegetables, cooked in garlic, oil and
tomatoes, served cold)

Tomato Monegasque
(Half a tomato filled with tuna fish, mayonnaise and
cibols, garnished with lemon slices)

Waldorf Salad
(Diced celery and russet apples with quarters of walnuts in
acidulated cream)

Rice Mexicaine
(Cooked rice with chopped mixed peppers and tomatoes,
in a French Dressing)

Jambon de Proscuitto en Cornet
(Proscuitto Ham rolled into tubes and stuffed with cottage
cheese and chives)

Salad a la Reine
(Batons of chicken breast, shredded celery, sliced beans,
tomatoes and mayonnaise)

Potted Shrimps
(Fresh shrimps cooked in clarified butter, lemon juice,
cayenne pepper and set when cold)

Bismark Herrings
(Herring fillets stuffed with raw onions prior to being
pickled in white wine vinegar)

Cole Slaw
(Shredded white cabbage, grated carrot and onion,
pineapple, sultanas in mayonnaise)

Pickled Lambs Tongues
(Lambs tongues pickled in brine, sliced and served on a
bed of salad with tomatoes)

The brislings, potted shrimps, pickled lambs' tongues and bismark herrings were bought in already prepared and then simply had to be dressed in the raviers, whereas all the salads were made fresh (all cooked vegetables were prepared and cooked by the vegetable chefs); indeed, they were often the unused cooked vegetables left over from a lunch or dinner time. Our job was to collate the salad ingredients and dress them in such a way as to stimulate the appetite by complementing colors, flavors and textures into each dish.

Hard boiled eggs were cooked by the box of three long hundreds (they were originally sold in long hundreds – one hundred and twenty eggs – to allow for any bad eggs in the consignment and ensure the customer got what they paid for, similar to the bakers dozen, but the customer was only charged for one hundred eggs). When I say cooked by the box, that is precisely what happened; everything went into the steamer trays and then into the steamers – the whole box full of eggs, and I do mean box!

They were cooked in this way because it would have taken too long to unpack three hundred and sixty eggs and place them into the trays, so the whole lot went into the steamer and when cooked, the porter power hosed off the very soggy remnants of cardboard. They still had to be peeled by hand though, all three hundred and sixty.

The final major component of our work was to prepare up to a thousand hot and cold canapés ready for the pre-dinner cocktail parties. The following were examples of the cold canapés used:

Sardines on triangles of toast with chopped parsley and cayenne

Smoked salmon on fingers of brown bread

Colored and flavored Philadelphia Cheese on Ritz biscuits

Piped liver pate on Ritz biscuits

Shrimp barquettes coated in aspic

Celery fingers piped with Roquefort cheese

Quails eggs on roundels of white toast, with aspic

Fingers of anchovies on brown bread with segments of lemon

Caviar on slices of boiled egg on Ritz biscuits

Cheese and pineapple hedgehogs (it was the sixties!)

A selection of the above were arranged upon a d'oyley on a round silver tray – approximately one hundred pieces per flat. A couple of cheese hedgehogs, most popular and fashionable at that time, were placed on the sides of the flat to give interest and height. The centre pieces were flowers, carved from a variety of vegetables and where appropriate, dyed in a variety of colors with food colorings. Once ready, the flowers were mounted on cocktail sticks (particularly the potato roses) and stuck onto half a large potato covered with lettuce or artificial ivy leaves. Many of these vegetable sculptures have since been popularized by Chinese and Asian cookery.

Examples of hot canapés were:

Small cheese tartlets (made by the bakers)

Chicken bouchees (pastry cases made by bakers)

Pineapple, cherries or mandarins wrapped in streaky bacon, grilled

Deep fried Scampi with a dipping sauce

Deep fried goujons of plaice with a dipping sauce

Homemade savoury sausage rolls (made by the bakers)

Angels on Horseback (oysters wrapped in bacon)

Devils on Horseback (prunes wrapped in bacon)

Welsh Rarebit on Ritz biscuits

A selection of the above were served on a dish paper on a round flat with a timbale full of cocktail sausages as a centre piece. Approximately one hundred pieces were assembled on the flat at a time. These trays were heated in a hotplate prior to service time.

I remember one evening when the chef was doing one of his rare quality inspections (normally when he was in a bad mood; why are chefs so temperamental?) and he came into the larder and his foot slipped on something. Fatal! Despite the fact that some thirty waiters were outside awaiting the completion of the canapés for immediate transportation to the numerous pre-dinner cocktail parties, which were about to start throughout the ship, the chef walked the length of the work bench with his arm outstretched, scraping all thirty flats onto the floor declaring that, "These are c**p and not fit for f*****g animals to eat! Do them again!"

With that he turned on his heal and walked out of the larder. The panic this caused was unbelievable! Chefs, waiters, porters... anyone and everyone rushed in to retrieve the canapés from the deck and started to rebuild the flats; however, only the piped canapés were actually redone all in about ten minutes instead of the two hours it would actually have taken, if we had redone everything. The biggest miracle was that none of the customers were ever ill! We were extremely fortunate that the hot canapés had not been taken out of the hotplate as they were too fragile to have survived being thrown onto the floor.

The head chef was a man who appeared to be in his seventies, but that may have been because we were at that age when anyone over thirty seemed very old. He was obviously of Irish descent as his name suggested; he was a very tall and an extremely thin man, who looked even taller when wearing his chef's hat (in those days the higher your rank, the taller your hat; whereas nowadays, different colour neckerchiefs are most commonly used to denote rank). He had a real beak for a nose, upon which he balanced his thick, horn rimmed glasses, but even these failed to hide the way his eyes rotated in his head in such a way that it gave the impression that he was watching you no matter where you were. The ways his eyes swiveled around in his head was the reason that everyone referred to him as the "flying saucer".

Nevertheless, his mere presence and the aura that surrounded him brought a feeling of enormous respect, which bordered upon fear and he certainly was not a man to argue with, irrespective of whether you were a member of the crew or a passenger.

As you would expect from a man in his position, he was one of the most knowledgeable and educated people that you could ever wish to meet; not only did he speak some thirteen languages (including several dialects) but he was so very well read that he was able to engage in conversations upon most subjects. Indeed, he relished the challenge of new topics that meeting new people brought. However, he was human (believe it or not) and had his weaknesses, especially his love for powerful motorbikes, particularly the British Norton bikes and the early versions of the American Harley Davidson. He loved nothing better than to don his black leather gear and ride off into the horizon once the ship had docked. No one ever knew where he went; indeed, no one seemed to know very much about the person beneath the "hat".

He also had a responsibility for all student cooks as well and he would meet with us for a minimum of one hour per week, irrespective of the pressure his job brought. During this time he would discuss our work, how we were managing and, more importantly, what we were learning. It was always the latter that he pressed us the most on and he would probe this aspect of our work, the most. Certainly, he would even personally arrange transfers to other sections of the kitchen if he felt we were not constantly being challenged, bearing in mind that we were normally students until we reached the age of twenty-one!

This broad based training, he believed, was the only way that top quality staff could be produced to protect the future of the Cunard Steam Ship Company. He had great faith in us and would always refer to us as his successors… statistically impossible as there were often up to eight of us and only one head chef's job, unless he believed we would inherit his job on a rota basis?

The biggest problem he faced was finding ways of keeping us motivated and keen to learn, week in week out. His solution was quite simple and effective – money! Every week he would send us down to his personal library, which was probably the largest collection of cookery books ever assembled by any one person. To ensure we used the time to best advantage, he promised us the equivalent of one week's wages to anyone who could find a recognised dish which he could not describe. We would read through these books, making notes and eventually we would whittle our lists down to one dish each with which to challenge the chef.

I can only ever remember one occasion when we found a dish which he was unable to describe fully and totally accurately, allowing us to claim the cash prize, as promised, and even then that was on a technicality, rather than finding something he did not know. The dish was Chicken Marengo, which historically is finished with a French fried egg (the egg is dropped into the deep fat fryer and turned quickly into a round shape using two spoons – a very skillful task). The chef said it was finished with a fried egg, which we argued to be incorrect! He eventually gave in and paid up. That was the only time I ever heard of anyone beating him and claiming the prize, which clearly spoke volumes about his knowledge and his ability to recall information.

An example of a typical First Class Dinner Menu, in full:

DINNER MENU

Juices: Grapefruit, Pineapple, Tomato, Orange

Chilled Grapefruit soaked with Kirsch
Chilled Florida Cocktail
Bluepoint Oysters on the Half Shell
Smoked Scotch Smoked Salmon with Capers
Beluga Malossol Caviar   Terrine de Foie Gras

Hors d'Oeuvre

Antipasto Italienn	Sardines in Oil	Chou: fleur Portugaise
Salade Orientale	Endive a la Grecque	Thon aux Capres
Hareng en Tomate	Brislings	Cornets de Jambon en Gelee
Roll Mops	Salade a la Reine	Potted Shrimps

Olives – Green, Ripe, Stuffed and Californian

Soups

Turtle Lady Curzon Crème Dame Blanche
Cold:Bortsch, Polonaise Gelee de Volaille

Fish

Fresh Scotch Salmon, Cucumber, Hollandaise Sauce, Parsley Potatoes
Fried Fillets of Boston Sole, Remoulade Sauce
Scampi, Newberg

Farinaceous

Gnocchi, Romaine

Vegetarian

Celery Hearts with Grated Cheese

Entrees

Escalope of Veal, Viennoise   Pouisson en Cocotte, Bonne Femme
Baked American and Virginia Ham, Glazed Peaches, Sauce Madere

Continental Speciality

Pintadeaux aux Cerises
Fillets of young Guinea Hens sautéed in butter and braised lightly in a wine and Cherry Sauce. Served under glass on a bed of Wild Rice and garnish with Morello Cherries

Joint

Roast Leg and Shoulder of English Lamb with Mint Sauce and Redcurrant Jelly

Sorbet

Champagne

Grill (to order)

Fillet Steak, Chasseur
Spring Chicken Saratogas   Pork Cutlets, Sauce Diable

Releve

Roast Vermont Turkey, Celery and Peanut Stuffing
(Compote of Cranberries)

Vegetables

Green Lima Beans Steamed Patna Rice
Garden Peas Sautes Fresh French Beans
Broccoli au Beurre Tomatoes farcies, Provencale

Potatoes

Boiled	Chateau	Creamed – Puree	Candied Sweet
		French Fried	

Cold Buffet

Roast Ribs and Sirloin of Beef, Horseradish Sauce

Roast Chicken	Oxford Brawn	Galentine of Veal
Rolled Ox Tongue	Pate Suisse	Roast Lamb, Mint Sauce
London Pressed Beef	Baked York Ham	Roast Duckling, Apple Sauce

Salads

Hearts of Lettuce	Sliced Tomatoes	Hawaiian	Fresh Fruit
Mona Lisa	Florida	Tossed Green	Chickory

Dressings

French	Swedish	Thousand Islands	Mignonnette

Sweets

English Plum Pudding, Brandy Sauce　　　Ananas, Stromboli

Coupe Royale　　　Chocolate Nut Sundae

Blueberry Cheesecake　　　Assiettes de Petits Fours "Queen Mary"

Ice Creams

Vanilla	Café Marron	Biscuit Praline (Hot Caramel Sauce)	Raspberry	Lemon

Savouries

Croute Ivanhoe　　　Welsh Rarebits　　　Diable a Cheval

Fresh Fruit

Apples	Plums	Oranges	Pears	Bananas
	Grapes	Ortaniques	Tangerines	Pineapple

Almonds, Figs, Raisins and Table Dates Assorted Nuts

Coffee (Hot or Iced)

SUGGESTED MENU

Pamplemousse au Kirsch

–

Tortue Lady Curzon

–

Saumon poche, Concombre, Sauce Hollandaise

–

Filet de Boeuf grille, Sauce Chasseur
Haricots Verts Sautes   Pommes de Terre Chateau

–

Pouding aux Prunes a l'Anglais

–

Panier des Fruits

–

Café

The Chef invites you to give him an opportunity to prepare your own favorite dish, whether it be a speciality of America, Europe or Eastern Cuisine. He merely asks that you give the head waiter sufficient notice to enable your order to be prepared to perfection.

The head waiter will also gladly offer suggestions and advice on dishes to suit your personal taste and, if you are on a restricted or special diet, to see that your requirements are met.

We student cooks did not fly off every time we arrived in the Big Apple; this was particularly true on those trips when one or more of our group were on leave, as this often meant there were not enough of us left to spread the costs of the hotel or taxi, which we quite often had to use on such trips. When we were not flying off, we always started our day with lunch in Woolworth's (we either slept until lunchtime or had to work until late morning). Yes, I did say Woolworth's; this was the best place both for a meal and to get value for money.

Each of their stores had a couple of horse shoe counters stretching out into the body of the shop, from which they served what we now know as fast food, but in the early sixties it was the latest of food fashions to die for! Indeed, there was often a queue for seats even in the largest of their shops. After lunch, we would then go to the "in place", Greenwich Village, to enjoy some fun locally, and we particularly liked to visit one of the many bars or clubs for which the area was famous.

We were, however, pre-warned about the gay bars and the sex clubs which were regularly frequented by the sixties version of the "lady boys", who were specifically looking for young and innocent boys like us. Naturally, we avoided such haunts like the plague, despite the realization that the stories which surrounded such places were grossly exaggerated to act as a true deterrent. Not that we were brave enough to test this theory ourselves, you understand!

On one occasion, when two of our group were on leave, Alistair, a young Geordie, who worked on the Sauce Corner (the section of the kitchen responsible for all main courses which were not roasted or grilled, together with all the hot sauces required by the rest of the kitchen) and I, went to a club in the evening. However, as there were just the two of us, we did not dare to risk going into the "village". Instead, we went to a club just off of 42nd Street, thinking that it would be safe, as we had been there on previous occasions.

We arrived fairly early in the evening to find the club was dead and almost empty, so we left and went to look for somewhere to get a drink and an evening meal before returning later on in the evening. After a relaxed meal we did return to the club to find that it had begun to fill up, with more and more youngsters arriving all the time and naturally, all the unattached guys took every opportunity to vet all the females as they arrived in the hope of having the first pick for a "dance partner".

This club always had a good selection of the latest music blaring out from the juke box, bearing in mind that the sixties were renowned for the quality of its innovative and exiting dance music, from both sides of the Atlantic. On this particular evening, one of these young ladies caught Ali's eye, so he quickly moved in on her and set about monopolizing her "dance card" for the rest of the evening. She did not really have a dance card; after all, it was the 1960s and not the 1860s! Being a tall, dark and I suppose, a somewhat handsome young man – not my type you understand – with what could be described as a muscular body, which he accentuated with the most up-to-date style in clothing, meant he always appeared to find it easy to attract members of the opposite sex and that night was no exception as he appeared to click straight away with this young lady, leaving me all alone at the bar.

After quite a boring evening, which I had spent alone in the bar admiring Ali dance with this young lady – he never even bought me a return drink – I decided that I had had enough and about midnight I decided to return to the ship. So I sought out Ali to see if he was going to come back with me; however, surprise, surprise, he said he would stay a bit longer and I remembered him winking as he said this, which I took to mean he was really hoping to strike it lucky and was anticipating going home with the young lady.

Mind you, I did not blame him, as she was rather gorgeous, if a little on the petit side.

She was about five feet six inches tall, with shoulder length blond hair which flicked up at the end to accentuate the shape of her face; her eyes were a fascinating steel blue in color and appeared to have the ability to look right through you without doing you any harm. I remember that she was wearing a bright red cocktail type dress which flared out provocatively just above the knee to expose two extremely shapely legs. This simple effect was achieved because the petticoat she was wearing, contained several concentric metal hoops which in turn, held the hemline of the dress off of her legs, which of course reflected the latest fashion craze. Naturally all of us hot blooded young males whole heartedly approved of any female style of dress which exposed the legs above the knees!

I also remember noticing that the wearer had to be extremely careful when sitting down as the whole front of the dress was prone to projecting itself up and over the head of its owner to expose the whole of the lower half of the body! Oh happy days, but it never happened that night, despite the ardent prayers of half the males in that club.

Anyway, I reluctantly left the club alone and jumped into a cab, which of course I had to pay for, and returned to the ship on my own. Even though 42nd Street was not far away from the docks, it was not safe to walk through this area at any time, never mind after midnight, as it was full of heavily armed gangs of youngsters who appeared to own whole blocks of the area (we now call this "Turf") –

straight out of West Side Story – and despite the fact that most of the gang members only seemed to be about thirteen or fourteen years of age, they were extremely dangerous, not to mention vicious.

Nearly every member of these gangs was heavily armed either with knives, knuckle dusters, razor guns or some other lethal weapon, which they were not afraid to use and I understand that they often did, purely for the fun of it and to break their boredom!

Indeed, even the local police went about in small groups, just in case and the police had their own guns.

We were always warned that if we ever found ourselves in such a situation, the best and by far the safest course of action was to take out our money and throw it as far away from us as possible and just hope the gang members scrambled to recover it, giving us the opportunity to run like hell! Whatever happened, you should never try to fight it out with these young thugs as you would always be the loser and almost certainly, one would get very seriously hurt, a story which is unfortunately reflected in virtually every dockland area throughout the world, even today, hence the necessity to depend upon taxis when venturing into working docklands. It has to be said that such areas were always well policed by New York's finest, but the gangs somehow always appeared to be one step ahead of them and avoided being caught in the act.

About three o'clock in the morning, the two of us sharing the cabin were rudely awoken by our cabin door being slammed open, accompanied by the sound of loud swearing, I jumped up with a start to see Ali standing there. He did not appear to be either hurt or drunk, just extremely angry.

"What on earth is wrong?" or words with a very similar meaning but less printable - I asked, still half asleep. He went on to explain that after I left, Carrie-Ann, which apparently was the name of the young lady I had seen him with earlier at the club, and after having indulged in some heavy snogging, she suggested they went back to her place, which apparently, was way out in New Jersey, for the rest of the night, and she even promised to run him back to the ship after breakfast the next morning, in plenty of time for the start of his shift.

He was eventually persuaded to accept her offer -it must have taken all of five seconds- and when they got outside he discovered that she was the proud owner of a beautiful red convertible sports car. Naturally, this was the icing on the cake and he thought all his birthdays had come all at once.

Having succumbed to her wishes, it was not long before they had left the streets of New York far behind them and were speeding off down the freeway towards New Jersey.

Some forty minutes later, they were safely ensconced in her beautiful Penthouse Condominium, where they immediately picked up where they left off in the club. He went on to explain that it was not long before his hands began to wander from behind her head, down her neck, to explore her upper body and her breasts. He was very much encouraged by the fact that he met no resistance to his manoeuvres. Ali remembered at the time, thinking that her breasts were a little on the small side, although that did not worry him unduly as he felt very confident that he was onto a good thing.

When he made a move upon the "other" lower part of her anatomy, she stopped him explaining that it was her wrong time of the month and if they continued they would have to have anal sex. It was only then that he became very suspicious, as he had never experienced such a deviation before and he had never heard any of his mates talking about the pleasures of anal sex (they appear to have discussed every other sexual position in the book) and so, whilst occupying her mind with a passionate French kiss, he gently ran his hand up her leg, over her thigh and under the front of her dress, where, to his surprise, he grabbed hold of the biggest pair of b******s imaginable! He could not believe it! He was almost physically sick!

He was so angry and shocked, that he picked *her* up by this newly discovered part of her anatomy and he physically threw her across the room, so violently that she thudded into the wall opposite. He was not sure if he had suddenly inherited the strength of Sampson or whether it was a manifest of his extreme anger, which allowed him to actually pick her up, never mind throw her. But somehow this was what happened. As she lay there, stunned on the floor, he found her handbag and removed her purse, and then helped himself to all of her money, which he then used to pay for the taxi back to the ship; after all, she had promised to get him back to the ship in time for his morning shift.

He went on to say that he would have taken her car and driven himself back to the ship if only he could have found the keys and if he had known exactly where he was. I listened in stunned amazement and could scarcely believe what I was hearing; after all, I had actually seen this "young lady" myself, and at no time did I even suspect that I was looking at anything other than an attractive young lady.

Really, if Ali had not been quite so quick out of the blocks, I may even have been interested in having a dance with her myself. Oh, lucky me! It was because of experiences like this that most of the crew never picked up women, especially when in New York as you just never knew what you were getting into.

I remember another occasion when Angus (you guessed it, the original genuine Scot, although he was from Edinburgh, which is said to be more like England than England itself!) and he always insisted upon wearing his kilt, which naturally featured his family tartan, not to mention his sporran and his skein do (a small dagger which fitted discreetly into his knee length sock) and I decided to try our luck star spotting. On the trip out, I had the dubious pleasure of serving a well-known young English rock star who was trying to break into the American market through personal appearances and the American release of his latest record and film. During one of our brief conversations, he had asked if I knew anything about the hotel he was staying at while in the Big Apple and despite not being able to help him, I did remember the name of this hotel and so, being at loose ends, we decided to go and see if we could meet him .

Upon arriving at the hotel reception, Angus simply asked which room Mr X was staying in, as he was expecting us; we were told that he was in the middle of a press conference, to which he replied that we had been invited and were supposed to be present, but unfortunately, we were running a little late. The receptionist immediately summoned a bell hop to escort us straight up to the room in question and when we arrived, his manager opened the door to be told by the bell hop that we were expected. The manager, who luckily I had never seen before, actually tipped him and thanked him for his assistance.

To our surprise, we were cordially invited in and given a glass of champagne. The formal part of the press conference was apparently over and the reporters were now enjoying the hospitality of a buffet and the champagne while getting to know Mr X personally.

Our arrival – especially Angus's as he was dressed in his usual kilt – quickly attracted the attention of the press, who immediately started to ask us questions, like who were we?

How did we know Mr X? What were we doing in New York? etc. So we blagged it, claiming we were old friends from a party in London a couple of years back and we just happened to be in the Big Apple on business and had just popped in to wish him good luck. I am not sure how welcome an addition we were for our host, as he did seem to have his nose put out of place when the photographers collectively asked for shots of the three of us together, luckily none of which were ever published, as far as I am aware.

Naturally, Mr X met thousands of people all the time and could not remember half of them, but he did say that we looked familiar (he failed to connect me and the Queen Mary, probably because I was not wearing my chef's uniform), and in an attempt to hide his own embarrassment, acted as if he did indeed know us and even remembered the party where we had met a few years previously, although he did admit he could not actually recall our names. He actually apologised for this; all I can think of was he did not want to look bad in front of the press. Consequently, we spent a very agreeable hour being feted by our host and the press, until it was time for him to leave for his Premiere at the cinema.

Before leaving, he asked if we would like to come along and see the film, and as we had nothing better to do, we accepted his kind invitation. Imagine our surprise when we were escorted down in the lift and outside to an awaiting 1960s version of a chauffer driven stretch limousine. We were then whisked away through New York to a cinema on 42nd Street.

When we arrived, there was a small crowd of about fifteen girls waiting outside the cinema, who appeared to spontaneously start to scream when they saw the limo arriving.

Apparently, they had been hired from "rent a crowd" and had actually been paid to be there to create a fuss, but unfortunately, this backfired when the three of us got out of the limo, as the girls did not have a clue as to which one of us was the actually the star whom they had been employed to scream at, so to be on the safe side, they treated all three of us as stars as we walked up the red carpet. It was not the Oscars but it certainly did feel good to actually have women scream at us for the first (and only) time, even if they had been paid to do it!

Nevertheless, the three of us went on in and watched the film together from the best seats in the house, plus we had a plentiful supply of free popcorn, ices and sodas. At the end of the film we made our apologies while Mr X was signing autographs and we discreetly vanished into the ether, in other words, we ran like hell. We tried to repeat this escapade on several other occasions, but with no success; whether Mr X actually sussed out what had happened and warned / complained to the hotel, we never did find out.

As for Mr X, he never did make it big in the States; apparently, they preferred some other home-grown guy by the name of Elvis Presley – you may have heard of him? He released quite a few worldwide number one records together with several hit films.

The problems for us students were not just restricted to the time we spent ashore; there was also serious dangers on board, especially for the unwary and despite all of the endless warnings we were constantly receiving, there was always someone who had to find out the hard way. Pete proved to be our exception. He was a small, eighteen-year-old, weasel-like lad, who came from Southampton and worked in the sauce corner with Ali. He was not the most popular member of our group, probably because of his tendency to be a know it all, who did and said extremely stupid things.

It would appear that late one night after we had all gone to bed, he found a card school, which turned out to be more than a card school, as they are reputed to have started to play the highly dangerous and illegal game of "Crown and Anchor", the worst game anyone could get involved in and it was the one game we were constantly and specifically being warned about.

Even to this day, I still do not know too much about the game, other than the fact that it is a game of dice which it appears you can never win but you can lose a fortune very quickly. It would appear that Pete stupidly allowed himself to get drawn into this game and it was subsequently rumoured that he duly lost a fortune, which was not helped by his stupid pension of doubling up his stake each time he lost in a desperate attempt to recover his losses and get himself out of debt. He must have been absolutely terrified as he had no possible way of paying off his reputed debt; indeed, it seems incredulous that he was even allowed to lose half of the sum he was rumoured to have lost. Surely, the people organising the game must have realised he was a student chef, as there were very few other crewmen of his age on board.

All we really knew was, at some time during the night, an hysterical Pete burst into our cabin desperately begging the three of us to lend him money – as much as possible. I seem to vaguely recall the amount of money he wanted, but I was somewhere between consciousness and the world of dreams and, even to this day, I do not know if that amount was part of a dream or reality. Well, naturally we were none too happy at being woken up and we all told him to clear off, little realising the dire consequences that appear to have resulted from our response.

Next morning when we woke up, we noticed that Pete's bunk had not been slept in and when we went up to the kitchen, there was still no sign of him. By nine o'clock we started to worry about him. Ali had covered for him by telling his boss that Pete was not feeling too good, and he had been up half the night being sick and so we let him sleep in.

We all got together, supposedly for breakfast, but in actual fact it was to discuss what we should do next; naturally, Ali was not too keen to say anything which made him out to be a liar as he was hoping to get promoted in the near future and did not want to jeopardise his prospects.

By lunchtime, we were frantic and collectively asked to speak to the sauce chef in confidence. We explained our concern about Pete's disappearance and shared the patchy facts, as we knew them, which in truth was very little. He immediately insisted we informed the head chef, irrespective of the consequences and so we did.

Before we knew what was happening, the Staff Captain and the bosun were down in the chef's office questioning each us individually. An immediate search of the ship was organised and repeated messages were sent out across the ship's tannoy for Pete to report to the chef's office at once. After two hours, there was still no sign of Pete and the Captain himself took personal charge of the search. All deck hands and off duty crew were organised into search parties for a meticulous search of the whole ship including the engine rooms, life boats, passenger accommodation and all state rooms etc. but without success. After four hours the search was called off. It was now early evening, almost eighteen hours since Pete was last officially seen, and quite naturally there were all kinds of rumours flying around as to his fate.

It was at this stage that all the staff who had used the Pig on the previous night, were interviewed by the ship's officers in an vain attempt to piece together what might have happened. I should reiterate that "Crown and Anchor" was officially banned from all British Merchant Ships at that time and so nobody would admit to either playing or seeing anyone play this game. However, is was known that there was a gang operating on board, but there was no concrete evidence to support this rumour. Gradually, crewmen began to detach themselves from any involvement in this disappearance and snippets of information started to appear anonymously in the suggestion box, which was there purely for the crew to use anonymously.

It became clear that Pete had discovered the whereabouts of a game of "Crown and Anchor" and had gone along, He had somehow managed to gain admission to this secret room, but it appears he was not content to purely be a spectator and it seems he was soon encouraged to join in playing, and before he realised what was happening, he was losing big time.

Rumour had it that it was not long before the organisers (reputedly stokers) closed his credit and started to demand their money. When Pete explained that he could not possibly pay up immediately, they became extremely menacing and gave him an hour to find their money or else. This must have been when he woke us up. It appears that the guys running the game had Pete followed to prevent him reporting the game and it was assumed that after the hour, the "or else" was invoked!

In the past, other crewmen welching on their debts had disappeared and it was an educated guess that they had been thrown overboard, to serve as a warning and to deter others from failing to honour their gambling debts. It was eventually assumed that Pete had also disappeared over the side of the ship sometime during that night.

The whole ship was gripped by an atmosphere of fear and everyone was so terrified that they would not even identify anonymously, the people who actually run the game. After all, it appeared that they had already committed a potential murder over an apparent debt, imagine what would happen to anyone who tried to inform upon them!

The American police were notified of this incident, but as the ship was British and it happened in International waters, they had no jurisdiction to conduct a full murder hunt.

When we returned to Southampton all the crew were restricted to the ship and prevented from going ashore until the British police had completed their own investigation and conducted a fruitless search of the whole ship for the "Crown and Anchor" equipment, in the vain hope of identifying the "murderers". Nothing was ever found and an inquest assumed that in the absence of a body, Pete had drowned at sea, probably at the hands of a person or persons unknown.

We did learn some valuable lessons from that experience, including never to gamble and never to ignore the warnings we were given by our elders, who were in a better position to understand the ways of this world, and to do so was at our own risk.

Once the police allowed us to leave the ship, all the student chefs went round to visit Pete's parents, which was the worst experience of my life as his parents were totally destroyed, not just by his death, but also by the absence of a body to bury. Something they never got over, despite having a memorial service some weeks after the inquest, which we all attended.

CHAPTER FOUR

When you are young, everything appears to be one big adventure and most of the time, those adventures are harmless. However, I remember one occasion when one of our so-called "harmless adventures" almost ended in total catastrophe. It was our free day during the summer when we were docked in Southampton and the usual gang were trying to think of something to do for a change, to break our boredom; you know what teenagers are like, they have a very low boredom threshold. The real problem was, we did not have enough time to go home because of our rotated shifts on duty.

Finally, we decided it might be fun to get the ferry to the Isle of Wight and even pay a surprise visit Johnnie's pub to see what it was actually like, after all, he had droned on and on about how wonderful it was for as long as we could remember. So, we got out of our chef's gear and into our civvies and set off to the nearby terminal to catch the ferry to the island. I remember it was a very hot day and so we had all decided to take our swimming costumes with us, in the hope that we would find a decent beach somewhere, which might give the opportunity to have a swim while we were on the island.

It was strange, because despite the proximity of the ferry terminal and the crossing being only some twenty minutes, none of us had ever been to the Isle of Wight before and so there was a certain element of excitement as we set off. We bought our tickets and we were very fortunate as there was a ferry there and waiting, enabling us to go straight onto the ferry for the short crossing, so good was our timing, that we did not even have time for a drink in the pier the café (there was no bar on the ferry anyway). Upon our arrival, we were delighted to discover that the pub was only about 200 yards from the ferry terminal and better still, there was a beautiful beach virtually just over the road. As it was a little early for the pub to be open (there were strict licensing laws in those days and the thought of all-day openings were merely fantasies) we all decided to go over to the beach for some sun bathing and swimming while we waited.

Naturally, when any group of young lads get together on the beach there is always a strong probability (or in our case a certainty) that there will be some horseplay, and this day was no exception, because once in the water, we all tried to drown each other. Or we were haring along the sandy beach, playing our own version of "British Bulldog", which meant we were shouting and screaming at each other... totally oblivious of the aggravation we were causing to the other holiday makers on the beach, that was until the police arrived!

Yes, you guessed it; one of the holiday makers on the beach had had enough and called the police, which in itself must have been difficult, as those were the days before the word mobile phone had not even been invented, never mind the actual phone and everyone still depended upon those wonderful old red public telephone boxes, which were on every street corner. God bless 'em. We were a little surprised that no one had approached us direct and simply asked us to calm down and have some consideration for the other people on the beach. Maybe they thought we were hooligans; come to think about it, we had been behaving like hooligans. In those days the police did not stand for any nonsense and they told us that if they had to come back because we could not behave ourselves, we could all expect to get a thick ear – and they meant it! In those dayseveryone had respect for the police; alright, I mean, we were all scared of them!

Accordingly, we quietly and sheepishly gathered our belongings together and headed for the pub, mumbling a feeble apology to any holidaymaker were met en route, although many of them gave us very strange looks and obviously had no idea what we were talking about.

None of us were not big drinkers, more accurately we could be described as steady drinkers; in other words, we took our time over each drink rather than gulping our pints down. This was not because we were extremely sensible youngsters, merely, we did not have enough money to spend the day drinking, nor did we have the large bladders essential to big drinkers. Also, at some point during the day, we had to buy our own lunches, which was a further drain on our resources.

Anyway, by about three o'clock, when the pub closed for the afternoon, we were all well fed and watered and having exhausted all the different games of darts we knew, we got round to discussing what to do next. God, we were a democratic lot in those days, discussing everything… it's a wonder we ever found time to actually get anything done besides discussing things that is.

Ali and I were both extremely keen and strong swimmers, so we wanted to go for another swim, whereas the others wanted to return to the ship, to prepare for a night out on the town, and it goes without saying that there was a genuine expectation of meeting some female company during the evening.

"If you guys are so keen on having a swim, why don't you swim back to the ship? We can always take your clothes back with us on the ferry," challenged Angus.

"Don't you think we couldn't, if we really wanted to," replied Ali, after all, we were young and invincible, so what could go wrong?

"Don't tell me, you're scared?" retorted Angus.

"Of course not, we just hadn't thought about it," said Ali.

"Look, the tide is coming in and will be behind you, which will make it even easier. It's not that far; you can even see our ship from here and so there is very little chance of you getting lost. I bet you a fiver that you couldn't swim all the way back anyway," said Angus. *A fiver*, that was the equivalent of a couple of days' wages!

I do not believe we were drunk; yes, we had had quite a bit to drink and were all very happy, but we certainly were not drunk, after all, we had to save some room for our evening vibrations. But the gauntlet had been thrown down and Ali was not one to refuse a challenge, and before I knew it, he had accepted the bet on behalf of us both.

Another fine mess you've got me into, Ali!

"Just one condition," said Ali. "You take our return ferry tickets and get us a full refund on it. That way we make some extra money."

It was at this stage that Colin, the student working on the fish section, realised that this was no longer a joke, but had become a serious proposal, and so he tried to take the sting out of the situation and to make us all see sense.

"Come on, lads, it must be over five miles back to the ship, you could not possibly swim that far… you'll never make it. Do you seriously want to risk drowning yourselves just to win a few quid?" he asked.

"Don't talk wet, the tide is coming in, so it will be behind us and will help push us in towards the ship. We probably will only have to swim about three miles and both of us could swim that any day, without even thinking about it," replied Ali.

"It is a bit far. I do not remember the last time that I actually swum that far... it was certainly some time ago," I interjected extremely nervously.

"Come off it, we often swim further than that, without even thinking about it," said Ali.

"Yes, I know, but we have been drinking and we had a full lunch, which we only finished half an hour ago. I was always told not to swim for at least an hour after eating and to allow even more time if we had had a large meal, and we certainly have eaten a large lunch, all three courses of it!" I whimpered.

"Well, if you are scared, I will go alone," replied Ali.

"It's not that I am scared, I just think we are being a bit reckless, risking such a long swim just to win a few quid. Also, we will be out there on our own and if we get into trouble..."

"Mike is right," interrupted Colin, "it would be different if we had a boat and so we could row back alongside you, just in case of any problems. But as it stands, you would be out there on your own."

"Yes, but the channel is not that wide, and if we were to hit problems, we could always float ashore on our backs. Simple," reasoned Ali.

When he put it that way, it all appeared so logical and I recall at the time that I found myself agreeing with him and asking, "What are we waiting for? Where do you want to start from? I think it would probably be better to walk along to the other side of the ferry terminal, that way we don't have to worry about being mown down by the ferries. Also, if we start over there, we will pick up the incoming tide quicker," I said pointing in the general direction of the terminal.

"Good idea," agreed Ali.

So we set off to look for a suitable starting place for our historic swim. We must have looked a motley crew, walking along the pavement towards the ferry terminal, two young hunks dressed only in swimming costumes, accompanied by two other youths, fully dressed and carrying more bags than a person living on the streets. Strange indeed, especially if you did not know what was about to happen.

We soon found our ideal place, far enough away from the terminal, to reassure us that there was no threat from the ferries. Ali and I decided that it would be best to swim in the middle of the Solent, as we would then maximise the benefit from the incoming tide.

Also, there were marker buoys for the shipping lane, which we could cling onto for small rests, if needed. Furthermore, we decided to alternate our swimming strokes between the front crawl and the breast stroke to preserve our energy and ensure our success; after all, this was not a race, it was a challenge, with a side bet to make it more interesting.

We said farewell to our colleagues and watched as they returned to the terminal to catch the waiting ferry. We looked at each other, as if to say, *what the hell are we doing?*

Whose idea was this? But neither of us backed out, not out loud anyway. Not that it would have been possible to change our minds anyway, as all our clothes, money and possessions had just set sail, on board the ferry just departed for Southampton!

It was at this point I asked Ali, "How are we going to get from the Solent to the ship? We don't even have our seamen's cards to prove that we are members of staff. We should have made arrangements to meet Colan on the other side."

"It's a bit late to think of such things now," Ali replied.

"We could go back to the pub and borrow some clothes and money, then catch the next ferry back," I said more out of desperation than expectation.

"You are brilliant, Mike. The pub is closed and even if it was open, they do not know us from Adam. Let's just get on with it and worry about what to do, when we arrive on the other side."

With that, we entered the water and set off at a steady pace – in other words, slowly. We started to swim out towards the marker buoys just like a couple of ducks; actually, we probably looked more like a couple of frogs as we were doing the breaststroke. As we swam, it became apparent that the tide was extremely strong as it rushed headlong up the Solent carrying us before it, or should that be down the Solent, I can never work out if a river goes downstream from its source or from its estuary? The incoming tide ensured that our progress was far quicker than it would have been without the friendly tidal current, however, we continually had to adjust our direction as the current often pushed us off course.

After half an hour of swimming we decided to take a rest on a convenient buoy, yes these things were big enough for both of us to climb up onto and actually sit on.

"How do you think we are doing, Ali?" I asked.

"Well up until now, I thought we were doing OK, but I think we may have a problem," he replied, pointing over my shoulder.

I turned around to see a large ship, which we later identified as the French liner, Isle de France, slowly gliding its way towards us and although it was only doing a few knots an hour, a ship that size, still created quite a wash, which was obvious from the way the marker buoys rolled about as she passed them. (Why is a ship always referred to as "she" anyway? Sorry to diversify.)

"What the hell do we do now?" I screamed, as sheer panic set in. "If we get caught in its wake, those propellers will make mincemeat of us. We haven't got time to swim for the shore and we will stand even less of a chance, if we get caught in open water."

"I think you are right," replied Ali. "Let's sit tight and just hang onto this buoy for dear life. At least that way we stand some sort of chance, whereas, as you say, if we get caught in open water, we will have no chance."

Time seemed to stand still and the approaching liner seemed to slow right down and it took forever for it to reach us, but reach us it did. As it pulled alongside us, there was no immediate difference in the water, but as it pulled past, the buoy started to gently rock in the water, then suddenly it started to buck violently, as the full impact of its propellers hit us. We have never been so scared in all our short lives as we sat there clinging onto the upper housing of the marker buoy. As it tipped from side to side it dunked us into the turbulent water, which made our situation seem even worse as we began to think that these buoys could even sink.

After what seemed an age, the waters around us slowly began to restore its decorum and our refuge began to stop its violent movements, much to our relief.

"I dread to think what would have happened if we were not on the buoy but in the open water between the markers? After all, if we were swimming we would have been oblivious of what was behind us," Ali said.

"It does not bear thinking about. But what do we do now? Should we risk going on or should we just head for shore and walk the rest of the way? After all, there could be other ships coming in on this tide," I blubbered.

"Look, if we swim ashore and try to walk back, how do we know if it will be possible to walk along the beach as the tide is in and there might not be any beach to walk on? If we continue to swim, I suggest we swim from marker to marker, that way we can stop and see what is behind us. If another ship does come along, we can always get onto the nearest buoy again and wait until it has passed us by," reasoned Ali.

Before we could arrive at a decision, we spotted a motor launch approaching us at high speed; luckily, it was nowhere near as big as the liner which had tried to drown us a short while before, although a lot smaller, its wash appeared much worse. As it got nearer, we realised it was the river police's motor launch and worse still, it was indeed heading straight for us. More trouble! Yes, we were indeed in trouble, because, the official river pilot on the Isle de France, had radioed the police to tell them about us and the possible danger we were to ourselves and shipping.

The launch slowed down well before it reached us, so as to minimise the wash and it slowly came alongside. A rope was thrown to us so we could anchor it to the marker buoy

and we were then transferred onto the launch. We were taken below deck to the cabin and immediately given large towels to dry ourselves and a warm cup of sweet tea,
which we readily accepted. As we drank our tea, one of the officers came in; he did not look best pleased. He introduced himself as the launch skipper and the ranking river policeman.

"What do you two comedians think you were doing, swimming in the middle of a busy shipping lane? Don't you know that you could have been killed? If you had been sucked into the props of that ship, you would have been fish food. Well?" he rasped.

It was at this point we finally grasped the seriousness of our situation and just how lucky we had been. So we explained the whole saga which, on recounting, seemed pretty pathetic, even extremely stupid and we felt it incumbent upon us to apologise for our stupidity. We were grateful when he accepted our apology, after giving us a damn good b*********g !

"What are we going to do with you now? Where did you say your clothes were?" he Continued.

"As we explained, everything is by now back on the ship by now and that was where we were heading for. I don't suppose there is any chance of a lift back to the ship, is there?"

Ali asked more in hope than expectation.

"Just what do you guys think this is, a water taxi? Don't you think we have better things to do than to nurse maid little snots like you," came the reply.

"I hope this is not a water taxi, because we do not have any money on us," whispered Ali, flippantly.

"That is neither funny nor helpful, sonny."

"Sorry," Ali whimpered.

"Normally we would bill you for this call out, especially as it was not the result of an accident, but simply your stupidity. I don't suppose you have a spare couple of hundred pounds hidden away in you lockers do you?" the policeman asked.

"Nowhere near," I replied. "We are just poor students."

"Well, I don't think we have any other option but to take you in and charge you with something then. The Court can decide a suitable punishment," he said.

Just then, another policeman entered the cabin and announced we had arrived.

"OK, lads, let's go!" we were told.

As we slowly climbed up the steps from the cabin, feeling both extremely stupid and frightened, we feared we were indeed heading for jail, but you can imagine our relief when we realised we were actually alongside the Queen Mary.

"You did not really think we could leave two half-naked morons roaming about the place, terrifying every old dear in Southampton, did you? Go on, clear off before I change my mind!" he said.

We did not have to be told twice; we were off the launch and onto the quay in the blink of an eye and we started making our way towards the ship.

"Oi! You two!" came a voice from behind. "Give us our towels back or we will do you for theft as well!"

Luckily, we managed to get back on board without further mishap. That night we did go into Southampton and we did meet some girls, one of which Ali eventually married, so this was our lucky day. Luckier for some than others, I suppose. All I know is that neither of us has ever tried to swim anywhere as part of a bet!

CHAPTER FIVE

As discussed previously, the Mary was one of the icons in Merchant naval History, reflecting a desire for luxury to offset the boredom often associated with travel and no expense had been spared in her outfitting to ensure the comfort and enjoyment of all her passengers.

The first-class state rooms and restaurants were of particular note, as all the walls and pillars were lined with various types of Italian marble, together with huge hand painted murals on each of the major walls. The state rooms included a library, reading room, smoking room, and a games/card room (casinos had not been legitimised at that time or I am certain one would have been included in the plans). I understand that originally a full sized snooker table was installed adjacent to the smoking room, but this proved to be impractical as the balls rolled around the table when the ship was at sea; no wonder I was never a ship designer as I would never have foreseen that happening, although I am surprised that they did not invent a similar game which used square balls, or perhaps they did, who knows?

The first-class restaurant was the most dazzling and opulent dining room ever built, and was the envy of the whole world. It had a capacity for up to 800 passengers, with sufficient room for silver or Gueridon service (silver service from heated trolleys) and still had room for a full dance band and for the guests to dance, which happened every evening, during dinner (except of course when it was extremely rough, the band still played but dancing was impossible). In those days, dinner was not just a meal but a social event, which went on all evening. It was often chaos for the waiters as they were just about to serve one of the courses to the meal when the band would play someone's favourite tune and all the passengers would suddenly get up from the table and start to dance!

The early 1960s was still a time when passengers dressed for dinner; men wore the formal black dinner jackets (white and other colours were unheard of), black bow ties which had to be tied by hand rather than clip on, cummerbunds were essential (black naturally), white dress shirts complete with jabots (yes I had to look it up as well – the frilly lace on the front of the shirt) and cuff links, patent black dance shoes were the also the order of the day. Sometimes it was difficult to tell the guests from the waiters as the latter wore long "tails" on Gala or party evenings.

The ladies were even more glamorous in there long flowing, sequined evening gowns, complete with tiaras and jewellery, all of which, were returned to their safes, at the end of the evening. I am surprised that many of the passengers did not employ security guards in their entourage, so valuable was their jewellery.

It was a period when the first-class passengers were all people who had grown up with wealth and consequently knew how to behave with the style and aplomb, as their surroundings deserved. However, this was soon to change with the advent of the nouveau riche, many of whom had come into money through successful businesses, but had not been educated to appreciate the finer things in life, in a relaxed manner. *No I am not a snob, just a realist!* This set of clientele were referred to by crew members as the "knotted handkerchief brigade", meaning they were more at home on Blackpool beach with fish and chips in a newspaper, than in the first-class restaurant of the Queen Mary.

Consequently, it was still a pleasure to serve passengers whose upbringing allowed them to appreciate and enjoy the lifestyle of the privileged classes.

Sailing days were always the busiest days of the week by far – both in Southampton and New York – as all boarding passengers were openly encouraged (at the time of making their booking) to invite their family and friends to join them on board to enjoy grandiose farewell parties. This was encouraged as it was a cost effective and ideal marketing opportunity to sell the ship to potential passengers of the future. In a highly competitive market, where every country with a maritime tradition had its own prestigious liners and people were still extremely patriotic, preferring to support their own countries liners - unless of course it could be proven that other options offered a superior service at a comparable cost.

Accordingly, every effort was made, not only to show off the ship, but to market the lifestyle and pampering that was inherent to such a voyage. Therefore, no expense was spared to show the ship off in its best light and every effort was made to ensure that everything was "shipshape and Bristol fashion" and that included the many extras which were on offer, including guided tours of the ship, and an opportunity to enjoy a live dance band in the restaurant (still an extremely popular pastime left over from the Second World War) together with afternoon tea. There were also promotional stands featuring very polished movies and photographs of famous passengers, who had used the ship in the past and they were often accompanied with letters of recommendation and thanks. Naturally, potential passengers were very impressed by the famous people and dreamt about meeting them or even sharing a dinner table with them; of course this never happened as the famous were always guests of the Captain's table, but why ruin their dreams before they had booked.

A major selling point was the Queen Mary's cuisine, which was world famous; unfortunately, it was not possible to include any of the working kitchens in these tours because of the hygiene and health and safety implications, so nothing has changed there then. Therefore, to compensate, the dining rooms were always dressed to maximum effect on these occasions, and every table was formally dressed with Irish linen table cloths, which were neatly starched and flowing to the floor so as not to expose any vulgar table legs! They were then dressed with solid silver cutlery and crystal glassware, all polished and gleaming; the table napkins were lightly starched before being folded into the most fantastic selection of shapes, the equal of which was not replicated in any other known restaurant, either on shore or at sea. The soft furnishings were brushed and manicured, and all the floors were polished until they glistened. Finally, there was the pièce de résistance, a twenty-metre buffet, which traversed the whole of the dining room – complete with a display of specially prepared foods and food models.

Featured in these displays, were cooked and ornately decorated joints of meat which, in reality, were often made from plaster of Paris models, shaped to replicate whole turkeys, saddles and crowns of lamb, whole sirloins of beef on the bone, whole gammons, chickens and game birds, complete with tail feathers recycled from real birds which had previously been used in the kitchen. These models were originally commissioned from professional artists/sculptors and then sealed with many coats of hard-wearing waterproof varnish, which allowed them to be washed off and used time and time again.

In order to reflect realism on these buffets, these models were firstly coated in a "chaudfroid sauce" (a white, pink or brown sauce which is lightly set with aspic jelly) and then artistically decorated with sliced and shaped vegetables, which were expertly put together to replicate flowers, flags, countries or other motifs. A final protective coat of aspic jelly both sealed in the decoration and gave the final product a gentle sheen, which then prevented drying out. They were presented on solid silver meat stands, which raised the joint off the serving dish, at an angle which best showed off its complex decoration. To retain the aura of realism, a few real slices of the appropriate meat were brushed with aspic and strategically placed around the artificial joints as an integral part of their decoration.

The finished dishes were then displayed on large, solid silver salvers, ornately decorated with silver filigree around the edges, then completed with a selection of vegetables sculptured into flowers (similar to those found today in restaurants featuring Far Eastern cookery) and finally a discrete salad garniture was added.

The fish dishes were more elaborate, as it is particularly difficult to produce realistic models of whole salmons, lobsters crayfish, turbots etc. Consequently, several variations were used to replicate the required article. The salmon was carved in a gentle "S" shape, to resemble the fish swimming, from a quarton loaf (a double length sandwich loaf), which was then allowed to go stale, before being deep fried. These models were then coated in a salmon pink sauce set with aspic, prior to being decorated with traditional items such as cucumber, lemon slices, radishes and prawns in their shells.

To further enhance the illusion of realism, miniature toy teddy bear eyes were inserted into the fish. One of the indicators of freshness in fish is the brightness and clarity of the eyes and so the toy eyes were essential to solidify this illusion.

Finally, they were dressed upon mirrored glass flats, complete with cooked and decorated halves of real salmon steaks and ornately carved lemons. Whole turbots were prepared in a similar way, carved from specially made loaves of bread, then they were coated in a white sauce enrichened with cream and set with aspic jelly. These products were often decorated with dyed potatoes carved into roses and mounted onto artificial stems to form miniature bouquets.

So realistic were these models that people actually believed they were in fact real fish dishes and I remember one particular occasion, when an American passenger, obviously intent upon showing off in front of his guests (I realise that it is difficult to believe as this is totally alien behaviour for an American. Damn, there goes any possibility of effecting any USA sales), demanded a slice from the displayed salmon.

Despite my best efforts to explain that this buffet had been on display for several hours and had had people breathing and coughing all over it, thereby rendering everything a potential and serious food poisoning risk, I even offered to personally go out to the kitchen and get a fresh portion of safe salmon for him. However, he was adamant that only a slice from the fish in front of him would suffice and, as the customer is always right, I asked him to take a seat while I cut a portion from the selected fish (I took great care to disguise the fact that this was nothing more than a portion of bread). It goes without saying that it gave me great satisfaction to see him show off in front of his friends by taking a huge mouthful, which he promptly spat out!

Naturally, he then tried to create a rumpus, shouting and screaming that he had been poisoned. Luckily for me, the Maitre d'Hotel had been watching this whole episode from the beginning, particularly as he had come to recognise potential problems before they developed, and as a result, he was able to step in as soon as the American kicked off.

"Excuse me, sir, may I have a word in private?" he interjected.

"Anything you have to say, can be said in front of my friends, they all deserve to hear your apology," came the arrogant reply.

"I would much rather we discussed this matter in private, as it would be much less embarrassing…"

"I don't care if you are embarrassed! I do not wish to discuss this matter in private," interrupted the American, smiling to his guests.

"Well, sir, if that is your wish," went on the Maitre D. "I witnessed the whole situation and I have to say that it was your insistence to have a slice from the buffet item which caused the subsequent problem. My colleague, the chef, did try to explain to you that the buffet food was not safe for human consumption; indeed, I distinctly heard him even offer personally to go and get you a fresh portion of salmon from the kitchen, but you chose to ignore him and it was you that insisted upon a portion from the buffet. Our staff are constantly and rightly reminded that the customer is always right. Consequently, he had very little option but to serve you with what you had demanded. I am sorry, sir, but you got what you asked for and if you were aggrieved by the outcome, I am afraid it is your own fault."

There was a deadly silence for what seemed like an eternity; it was actually a few seconds, before the American burst out laughing: "You are absolutely correct," he went on, "send the young man over so that I can apologise personally to him." It transpired that his apology consisted of a ten dollar tip (or seven pounds in real money – almost whole week's salary), which of course I graciously accepted.

The lobsters we used were real shells which had been emptied, scrubbed, coated with a clear sealant (varnish) and then filled with slices of lobster made from plaster of Paris.

This was coated with mayonnaise and decorated prior to being dressed on solid silver flats with a salad garnish. Alternatively, they were covered with breadcrumbs and lightly browned in a hot oven. The crayfish were real, but they were cooked and sealed with a varnish before being hung on a shellfish tower (circles of silver, which decreased in size as they went up) and the gaps were then filled with picked bunches of parsley and lemons. Naturally, they were used several times before being discarded.

To complete the main courses, raised meat pies were made, using an artificial, non-food filling of course and, once again, to give realism, glazed slices of real pies were arranged around the edges of the silver flats.

To complete the savouries, a selection of some ten to fifteen different mixed salads (yes, Folks, these were actually real; probably because no one had found a way to simulate such dishes!) were produced and displayed in appropriate dishes as they were an essential part of any buffet. As you would expect, there was always a magnificent centrepiece, which was normally an ice sculpture, usually of an animal such as a swan, a variety of a cat or even a bear. To create such a masterpiece, involved a couple of hours working in a walk in deep freeze with no more than a saw, hammer, chisel, blowlamp and a bag of salt which were used upon a solid block of ice some two foot cubed, whereas nowadays they use a chainsaw to give the basic shape and finish off with chisels etc.

My first attempt to carve a swan on my own, started off brilliantly. I had entered the ice station equipped with my duffle coat, scarf and gloves and I had successfully sawn the crude shape of the swan without too much problem. I then set about carving the detail, again, I thought, without any serious problem. Then came the time to effect the fine detail, particularly ensuring the neck was nice and slender. This is normally accomplished by lightly waiving a blowtorch up and down the neckline and then finally rubbing it down with salt – the secret is always to quit when you are ahead and not to keep striving for perfection. After two and a half hours, I forgot my own advice and continued to rub the neck with the salt, until it happened... yes you guessed it, the top of the neck and the head tilted to a jaunty sixty degrees! My swan suddenly looked like a creature that had spent the last two days trying to drink a brewery dry! Even its facial expression was that of a drunk! There was no ice carved centrepiece that day, for some reason, the chef did not see the appeal of my masterpiece.

The sweets were the biggest "cheats" of all; the gateaux and charlottes were in reality, decorated drums of wood! The three-tier wedding cake, in the glass case, complete with extremely complicated and intricate run out icing (it goes without saying that it would have been impossible to duplicate such a complicated masterpiece every other week, there just was not enough time, hence the use of the glass case, which prevented discolouration) also concealed wooden drums in their centres. The mousses and bavarois were merely coloured creams set with gelatine and decorated.

The pulled sugar work, was also exhibited in air tight glass cases, as they were real and the slightest ingress of damp could destroy the whole display. So good was the quality of this work that it always attracted a great deal of attention, especially when presented as a fruit basket or flower basket, as they looked so real (even the woven baskets were made from sugar). Quite often the pastry cooks would try to compete with our ice carvings, by producing pastry margarine or lard carvings, a much easier medium to work with as it did not melt and any mistake could be easily be rectified. Consequently, they were able to produce a far wider range of animal carvings than we could ever produce from ice. Their repertoire included, large cats, such as lions or tigers, dancing bears, horses, deer and even a polar bear with its cub, which of course made our humble efforts look pretty tame.

Finally, there was an exotic but finely detailed model; for example, a Greek temple or a typically English country cottage. This appealed to the American market, and it was made out of shortbread, measuring some three feet wide by two feet deep and two feet high. It was complete with sheet gelatine stuck over the holes in the walls to represent windows and inside there was a battery connected to a miniature lighting system which lit up the whole cottage. These cottages even had their own garden, a typically English garden, which typically comprised of set green jelly for a lawn with small marzipan flowers. All this was presented on a huge mirrored flat and because of the weight and size, it took four people to carry it into the restaurant where it had a table all to itself.

As you may have guessed from the above, it was part of my job to be present in the dining room to explain or discuss the food during the display times. I was also responsible for ensuring that the display always looked fresh at all times and if this was not the case, to rectify the problem.

Problems were thankfully a rare occurrence, but did unfortunately happen. On one occasion, the heat from the overhead lights started to melt the green jelly garden lawn, and as a result, the shortbread walls of the house stated to go green, and this green slowly worked its way up the walls (it resembled a bad case of rising damp). Although I did notice that this was happening, a very talkative and persistent passenger prevented me from doing anything about it, not that there was much I could have done. All of a sudden there was a loud "plop" and the whole house collapsed in upon itself, splattering green stained debris all over the place!

I immediately made my excuses to the customer and rushed out into the kitchen to seek the help of the head patissier, Hans by name, an eighteen-stone monster of a man from Austria, who grunted more than talked. However, he was an extremely talented practitioner, and upon seeing the mess in the restaurant, realised that all his display was completely wrecked beyond repair. This meant that everything not in a display case would have to be discarded immediately, which in turn, meant that everything would have to be replaced from scratch or replaced with real sweets which had been prepared for that evening. If this was the case, his team would have to start work immediately upon replacements, an impossible task He simply went bananas, but luckily there weren't many guests present in the dining room. All of a sudden, he picked up the largest knife he could lay his hands on and started towards me. I believe he said something about chopping my head off, but I did not hang around to ask him to repeat himself; instead, I simply took off in the opposite direction as fast as my legs would carry me.

Luckily, because of his size, he could not move very fast, but I have to admit, he did have stamina and every time I stopped to catch my breath, I could hear his laboured breathing following behind me. At the time, it seemed as if he chased me all over the ship, but it was probably only for about fifteen minutes. In desperation, I decided to try and make my way to the head chef's office to seek sanctuary and with my limited knowledge of the ship, I eventually found my way to one of the external decks, which allowed me to get my bearings and I was able to find my way back to the kitchen. I wish that I was not being chased by a madman as I would love to have seen the faces of the passengers and staff as firstly I hurtled passed them and a few moments later, by a huge asthmatic chef, wielding a chopping knife, came lumbering along, gasping for breath and trying to utter obscenities in German! Luckily, he failed to catch me and the head chef was already aware of the situation and was on hand to calm Hans down – most probably he prevented the poor guy from having a heart attack!

It was several days before I dared to approach Hans again to make my peace, but I eventually plucked up the courage and, armed with a pint of his favourite drink, I did manage to apologise and explain what had happened. When he heard what had happened, he actually laughed and after this episode we became quite good friends and he would often give me private lessons in the skills of the patissier to help me to develop my pastry skills.

It should be apparent by now that Hans had quite a short fuse and this came to the fore on another occasion. Each evening, the pastry section would prepare thousands of petit fours to finish dinner and these would be placed on silver flats for waiters to collect when ready. The only problem was that each time someone went past the service counter they would steal one of these sumptuous sweets, which infuriated Hans.

One evening he made up a batch of chocolate truffles and laced them with pepper, or should I say he made them with pepper, they were that strong! He placed them on the flats closest to the counter in readiness for the secret chocolate thieves and it was not long before the first person struck; you have never heard such a furore of coughing and spluttering, but he dare not say anything to Hans. This continued to catch unsuspecting thieves for the rest of the evening. However his plan backfired, as the unsuspecting waiters started taking the trays, including the peppered chocolate truffles, into the restaurant for their passengers.

Pandemonium broke out as soon as the unsuspecting passengers greedily tucked into the contaminated chocolates, they started coughing, spluttering and spitting out the offending chocolates. But of course not all of the petit fours were laced with pepper and naturally some passengers enjoyed there sweets, which totally confused the dining room staff. In the end, all petit fours had to be recalled and disposed of as there was no way of identifying the contaminated items. Naturally, there was hell to pay when the chef discovered what had actually happened.

The other aspect of the sailing day's magnificent show was the floral display. The full time "on board" gardener not only tended to the plants in the state rooms and luxury suites, but also made up exquisite displays for all the buffets, the posies for the dining room tables, plus the bouquets for the inevitable birthdays or anniversaries which took place on a daily basis. All of which were works of art in their own rights and how he managed to retain the aromas of the plants and flowers despite having been at sea for up to five days, was not only incredible, but also, a well-kept secret.

CHAPTER SIX

In the 1960s, homosexuality was illegal in mainland Britain and as a consequence, many homosexuals elected to pursue their careers at sea, where their sexual preferences did not infringe any laws. As a result, there were a substantial number of homosexuals and transvestites working on board most ships.

The "Queen" of the Queen Mary was a person by the name of "Aggie" (a name apparently derived from his initials), who worked as a waiter in the first-class restaurant.

"She" (as she preferred to be known as) was five feet ten inches tall and weighed about sixteen stone, which caused her to sweat profusely most of the time. She was almost bald with thin wisps of hair brushed over the top of her head, reminiscent of a famous English footballer prominent in the early to mid-sixties. She thought her Roman nose made her look distinguished, but this was not the case as her nose seemed to dominate her face in a grotesque manner, rather than enhance it.

Nevertheless, she was a superb waiter, with a tremendous personality, which presumably was why she was able to keep her job. Indeed, passengers even asked to be seated on her station, however, she expected an "introductory tip" before she would even start to serve anyone (a custom that was common in those days in the better circles) and if they forgot, or even if did not know about this custom, she would totally ignore them and would simply refuse to serve them. On one occasion, the head waiter had to ask another waiter to serve a couple who had not tipped Aggie, and as a consequence, were being ignored.

Accordingly, they summoned over the head waiter to enquire as to why Aggie was not serving them, who told them she was very busy that morning only to turn round to see her sitting down doing nothing at that precise moment. Guess what? The couple did not believe him and he was forced to explain that they had forgotten to tip her. The passengers were desolate, not by the rejection, but by the fact that it was their negligence that was responsible for the problem They immediately rectified this situation and Aggie resumed service immediately... well, after warning them not to forget in the future!

Every morning, prior to turning to, Aggie would commence her day with a large glass of neat gin (or two), after which she would inspect her fellow waiters' dress to ensure that they were up to the standard of the first-class restaurant and it was not unusual for her to sew on buttons or to adjust their dress in some other way... all in the best possible taste, of course. As a consequence of her early morning liveners and the volume of drink consumed the previous night, it was not unusual for her to place both her hands on the customer's table, usually, to steady herself. Her first sentence would often be: "What do you old crows want for breakfast this morning?" and she would stagger off to collect their meal, often returning with completely the wrong dishes, but no one ever complained. Despite her obvious drink problem, Aggie certainly knew how to play the passengers and thereby maximise her tips.

Every morning she would watch which page they turned to first when reading the on board newspaper and the following morning she would be able to engage them in a subject she knew the passengers were interested in; for example, if the lady read her horoscope first, she would read the stars before they arrived next day and begin by saying she was glad that her star sign was not X as the forecast was so bad, and for the men, her opening comment was along the lines of, "Did you see the price of the winner in the three o'clock horserace at Ascot? I would love to have had a pound to win on that." Naturally, such opening gambits endeared Aggie to her customers and ultimately ensured her next tip was the largest one possible.

In the evening, after work had finished, Aggie and her entourage would glide down to the Pig (the bar for non-officers on the poop deck of the ship) dressed in the most beautiful evening attire you have ever seen, including jewellery and a wig, all of which made Danny La Rue look like a very poor imitation, probably because everything they wore had been handmade to order by New York's finest couturiers. As one would expect, their entrance was always timed to make the greatest impact and was normally greeted by a chorus of cat calls from the assembled crew, usually "here come the prostitutes", to which Les Dames would respond with either "you substitutes are only jealous" or "don't knock it until you have tried it", or "are you scared to try it in case you like it". Naturally, this was purely light-hearted banter, with no offence being taken by either side.

Despite all her make-up and refinery, Aggie still abused the privilege of being ugly; in fact, I think she was one of the most ugly men I have ever met, although no one would ever say this to her face. Aggie's partner was an ex-Mr Universe contestant who still took great care to look after his body with a rigid fitness regime, and how he managed this on a ship with no gymnasium, we never knew. The constant use of a tanning lamp, completed the look which made him the envy of many a crew member, who could only wish they could look like him as they most certainly would have been fighting off the women when they went ashore.

Every trip, Les Dames would put on a show for the crew which comprised of a selection of the latest songs and dance routines from the shows and although such performances were totally spontaneous and lasted only thirty minutes at the most, they were always keenly anticipated and thoroughly enjoyed by everyone in their audience, as this was the only form of live entertainment available while at sea.

The surprising thing about the Les Dames was the fact that they never tried to convert anyone to their way of life, not even us young student cooks, who must have ranked amongst the most naïve youngsters ever to have signed on to this ship! Indeed, we certainly would never bend over to pick up any money we may have seen on the floor, irrespective of its value, probably because we believed the stories about the golden rivet and we never dared to take any chances. To be fair, I was told by other crew members that Les Dames were extremely pleasant to speak to and were very generous in buying drinks, as they always appeared to have plenty of money.

However, they were often the targets of genuine abuse and physical violence when they went ashore; consequently, they were always met by chauffer driven cars whenever and wherever we docked, which whisked them off to who knows where. Although we never did find out where they went to when in New York, besides the obvious visits to the high class shops of course, but it was rumoured that they owned a condominium in the city, which they used when in town.

There was one infamous occasion when their whereabouts were known. We were in New York and because of the ship's late arrival, the crew's time ashore was restricted to the bare minimum of two hours each and as a consequence nearly everyone simply went over the road to the bar which was used exclusively by our crew when we were in town. Les Dames joined us, all dressed up in their Sunday best, but unfortunately they were seen entering the bar by the crew members of the SS United States, an American passenger liner which was always in New York at the same time as us and docked in an adjacent berth. It was not long before a posse of their crew came a calling, intent upon expressing their disgust at the behaviour of Les Dames; apparently, they did not have homosexuals or transvestites on their ship. Yes, you guessed it, an almighty fight then ensued between the two crews which included Les Dames, and I was told that Aggie's boyfriend inflicted a fair amount of pain upon anyone who attempted to molest Aggie.

It was not long before the New York's finest arrived and they simply manoeuvred everyone outside and then surrounded them, allowing the fighting to continue. Finally, the police began to pluck people off the scrum and subjected them to a swift blow on the head with their night sticks. When an onlooker was heard to ask why they were not arrested, an officer explained that when the recipients recovered consciousness they would not feel like continuing to fight. Also, if they were arrested, the officers would have to attend court in their own time and naturally, they avoided as many arrests as possible, preferring other more instant methods of justice.

The saddest part of this episode was the fact that most of Les Dames' Sunday best was completely ruined; dresses were torn, wigs were lost or destroyed, jewellery was lost or stolen, fingernails were broken or ripped off, and false eyebrows were lost or reportedly, even eaten!

But it did not end there; both ships were held responsible and were ordered to pay for the damage to the bar before either ship was allowed to sail. Consequently, all members of the crew who were subsequently identified were logged and summoned to appear before the Captain to account for their actions and to face a charge of bringing the good name of the ship into disrepute, charges against which, there was no defence. As a result, they were all fined a month's salary, which was duly recorded in the ship's log book. It was not surprising that Les Dames were the first to be identified and fined, just to add insult to their injuries. Furthermore, a Cunard Law was, anyone displaying visible marks caused by a fight were banned from working in any public area so as not to upset the passengers.

Subsequently, any member of the crew found to be in this position, had to work behind the scenes doing more menial tasks, including washing up or peeling potatoes, until their wounds healed. Naturally, their wages were temporarily reduced to the same level paid to those members of the crew who were specifically employed to perform these tasks. Such draconian actions were normally a very good and effective deterrent, even though several crew members did evade identification and punishment.

Occasionally, there would be pre-arranged football matches between the various sections of the ship and Aggie always volunteered to be the "sponge" person. This involved dispensing primitive first aid to anyone getting injured, usually by plunging a sponge into iced water and then down the front of the injured player's shorts! AGGIE proved to be the most successful first aider ever, probably because the sight of sixteen-stone of pure fat wobbling towards you, like some huge walrus, whilst you are lying prone and defenceless on the ground, arouses every ounce of self-preservation instincts one can manage and despite the pain, a miraculous recovery occurs! Although it has to be acknowledged that her sexuality may, possibly, also have aided recovery and to my certain knowledge, Aggie never actually succeeded in running on fast enough to actually place her sponge down the front of anyone's shorts! Nevertheless, she still religiously turned up to matches, both to support the players and to administer first aid if required.

On one occasion, one of the teams was short of a player and Aggie actually volunteered to play – as long as she could play in goal – an offer which was gently declined and a substitute was quickly found as none of the team had any desire to either have her in their changing room or sharing their communal bath after the game.

But Aggie's football story did not end there because at another game in New Jersey, she became the first "sponge" person ever to be sent off and suspended from attending the following three games. It all started when one of our players appeared to get quite seriously hurt and before the referee could blow his whistle to stop play, Aggie had started her run across the field of play, which naturally upset the referee. Accordingly, he blew his whistle and waved at her to get off the pitch. Her response was to ignore him and to continue towards the injured player.

Eventually, the two came face to face beside the prone body of the injured player, who was still writhing about the ground in agony – he must have been hurt to still be on the ground when Aggie actually reached him. An almighty row ensued between the referee and Aggie, concerning the latter's right to be on the pitch before the referee had invited her on and, come to think of it, I do not actually remember anyone actually attending to the poor injured player, he just seemed to have been forgotten. The referee continued to insist that Aggie could only come onto the field of play when authorised by him, namely waved on, and as this had not happened, she must leave the pitch until called on. Aggie replied that he, the referee, was, at least useless, but more likely, totally incompetent and therefore wholly incapable of being put in charge of a bike never mind a football match. You will appreciate that the language was somewhat different to this and I have merely paraphrased the exchange between the two!

By this time both teams had gathered around both Aggie and the referee to express their opinions, but they soon retreated when Aggie took her bucket of iced water and promptly tipped it over the head of the defenceless referee, leaving the bucket wobbling about upon his head! The last official act in that match, was the sending off of Aggie by a bedraggled and shivering referee, who then abandoned the match prior to dashing off to a hot shower – not that we minded as we were losing 3-1 at the time! A week later, the Staff Captain suspended Aggie from attending the next three matches, irrespective of where they were played.

This proved to be a major disappointment as the company decided to pick a goodwill touring football team, complete with all the essential support staff, to tour the world playing exhibition games. Aggie was banned from participating in this venture because of her recent indiscretions, much to the relief of us players, particularly as we often had to share communal dormitories!

This touring team was made up of genuine Cunard staff, who like myself, were borderline professional standard footballers and we were strengthened by four recently retired professional footballers, all of whom were either English or Scottish International players. The tour started in Italy, where we played pre-season friendlies against Naples, Inter Milan and Roma; an impressive selection of opponents and all of whom fielded virtually their first team as we played in their stadiums, all of which were at least half-full of fee paying spectators.

In the first game, we played quite well in the first half and went in only 2-3 down and whereas the Italians (unknown to us) were given oranges as their refreshments, we found a couple of crates of beer in our changing room! Naturally, we could not refuse such generous hospitality and we eagerly finished the lot in the ten-minute break. As you can imagine, this beer had a telling effect upon us. I seem to remember some of our team playing as if they were actually drunk, and if the truth be known, they probably were, whereas the rest of us had the beer sloshing around in our stomachs throughout the whole of the second half, which had the effect of reducing our performance to a farcical display, which ended up in a final score line of 2-9! Yes, we conceded six goals in the second half, not that some of our team saw many of these goals through their bleary eyes!

This was the one and only time we fell for our hosts' dirty tricks as we certainly learnt from this most demeaning experience; yes, thereafter we actually refused the half-time beer and asked for oranges and/or a cup of tea, although it has to be said that we did keep the beer for when both of the remaining games had finished! As a result, we managed to draw our second game, before losing our final match by the odd goal in nine.

Our next destination was Germany where we played three of their premier league teams, (namely Hamburg, Dortmund and Munchen Glad Bach) in pre-season friendlies. Our Italian experience taught us a lot and paid dividends, and as a result, we were much more successful in these games, winning one and drawing the other two. We also played representative teams from the German Steamship Company, SS Hamburg and the SS Bremerhaven; the French Steamship Company (actually it was a team solely from the SS Isle de France), and finally the Italian Steamship Company, the SS Vasco da Gama and the SS Michael Angelo, all of whom we beat quite comfortably.

Finally, we flew to New York where we played three First Division English clubs (this was the equivalent of the Premiership, for you younger readers!) in warm up matches prior to their participation in the Inter Cities Cup. These games were rather strange as a condition of our being allowed to play such illustrious opponents was that we had to play in our plimsolls (the equivalent to the trainers of today). We were warned against strong or slide tackles to ensure that there were no injuries to any of the all stars, although I do not believe our opponents were given the same instructions, as several of our team went off injured! The boots were hard leather with dubbin and the ball was laced up leather! Once again we had mixed fortunes, winning one, drawing one and losing one game.

As you can imagine, this was a fabulous three months which we all thoroughly enjoyed and we all wished that this tour could have gone on indefinitely, but this was not to be and we all returned to our ships with some fantastic memories and souvenirs which no money could buy. I just wish I had kept the autographs which I collected, they would be worth a fortune now!

Upon my return to the "Mary", I was sent for by the head chef, who had both good news and bad news for me; the good news was I had been promoted to the post of extra hors d'Oeuvrier (deputy to the head hors d'Oeuvrier). This was quite remarkable as one was normally a student until you were twenty-one years of age, whereas I was a student for only ten working weeks, if you excluded the football tour! I was later told that the only person to be promoted quicker than me was the current catering superintendent for the whole of Cunard and his promotion was immediately after World War II when apparently skilled staff were in short supply The bad news was there was no vacancy for such a post on the "Mary" and consequently I was being transferred immediately to the SS Mauretania for Mediterranean and world cruises. I was given three hours to gather all my belongings together and make my farewells prior to catching my flight to Naples in Italy to join my new ship.

I remember that the flight to Italy was both extremely long and very uncomfortable, mainly because I was travelling alone and had no one to speak to and also the weather was none too kind and so the plane rocked and rolled all the way. Remember, this was over forty years ago and the planes were nowhere near as good as they currently are, they did not even have on board movies to watch!

As I arrived at the entrance to Naples docks, I was immediately besieged by locals sporting what I can only describe as the trays worn by the cinema usherettes in days gone by, to sell ice creams. However, the ice creams had long since been replaced with knuckle dusters, flick knives, razor guns, coshes and other implements of violence... all of which were for sale! Unfortunately, these very vendors and their friends used these very same weapons every evening to attack anyone they found speaking English.

Apparently, this was a direct result of a long running feud between the locals and members of the American fleet, who were also based in Naples. Indeed, I am led to believe that there had been several deaths on both sides and innumerable serious hospitalised casualties, since this "war" began and such fights were a nightly occurrence.

Unfortunately, the Italians did not have a sufficiently high standard of education todistinguish between the Americans and we British sailors and we were quite often attacked as well.

Early one night I went to a bar to await my new shipmates to finish their shift and join me so we could go out together. This bar was down four steps from the pavement and it was not the type of bar which I was used to in New York as it was very primitive in its décor; it had no jukebox, simply the sound of local music being blasted out by a wireless, which had its volume turned up to the maximum. There was no dance floor, neither were there any local women present. I remember thinking that it was a very strange place to choose as a meeting place. Anyway, as the evening progressed, none of my crewmates turned up; not that this was strange as it turned out that I had gone to the wrong bar! But not knowing the Naples I decided to wait.

As the evening went on I noticed another young guy in the bar was an American and it was not long before we got into a conversation as he was also on his own. He turned out to be a National Service sailor, serving on board the aircraft carrier Wasp, which was part of the Seventh Fleet based in the Mediterranean. It was a pleasant meeting and the evening just slipped by as we became more engrossed in our conversation.

Then, suddenly it happened; as I remember it, it was just after eleven o'clock and there were only half a dozen people left in the bar, when two youths dashed down the stairs and stood in the doorway examining the patrons left in the bar. They left just as suddenly as they had arrived. Gene (yes, that was my newfound friend's name; apparently, his father loved Western Films and in particular one cowboy called Gene Autrey) became very agitated as he knew these locals were part of a gang looking for American sailors to beat up and he was certain that we had been identified. If this were the case, the gang were now outside awaiting the bar's closure and our exit.

As you can imagine, I was somewhat shaken by this news. You could say there was soon a dark brown smell wafting around the bar, but I do not believe this was the reason why the locals who were in the bar, quickly finished their drinks and left. The departure of the last two left us feeling extremely vulnerable and we tried to ask the bar owner if there was another exit we could use, but unfortunately he did not speak English. So we decided to see if there were any young Italians hanging around outside and we gingerly walked up the four steps to the pavement, but by the time we reached the second step, it became obvious that our worst fears were justified, as there was a group of some six or seven young men standing opposite to the bar, openly displaying the fact that they were indeed armed! We quickly retreated back down the stairs to the sanctuary of the bar; for some reason the gang were loath to come into the bar to get us and they appeared quite happy to wait outside for us.

It was at this stage that Gene came up with the idea of keeping the barman sweet, so he would not close, before the American Liberty Lorry came around to collect their sailors from all the towns bars at midnight. Keeping him sweet meant spending money and all the time this was happening, we felt we were safe. As luck would have it, our bar was one of the first to be emptied. just before midnight to nightstick wielding MPs came down the stairs ordering all American sailors out and onto the lorry. Gene jumped up, dragging me behind him, whispering to me not to speak under any circumstances. He made for the door making sure that he did not let go of me for one second. The Italians were still there and when they realised what was happening and the fact that their prey was slipping through their fingers, they began to throw stones at the Liberty. However, they soon stopped when the MPs drew their side arms and pointed them in the vague direction of the stone throwers; instead, they turned on their heels and ran off, shouting what we assumed were obscenities as they went.

Our – or rather Gene's – plan was quite simple: just pretend to be a sailor until we got to the docks and then just slip away to join my own ship. Unfortunately, by the time we reached the docks, the lorry was jammed packed with the dead and the dying from the effects of alcohol over-indulgence, that extra MPs were mustered at the dockside to assist everyone onto the cutter, which took us all to the Wasp! Yes, I do mean all of us. I was manhandled with the rest of the crew onto a cutter and before I knew it I was on my way to the Wasp!

Guess what? I was experiencing that dark brown smell again! What the hell was I doing here? Why did I listen to a guy I had only known for a couple of hours? Why did I not just speak to the MPs in the bar and simply ask for their help? What a mess, and worse was yet to come. As we had reached the stairs leading up to the American Aircraft Carrier, Wasp, I spoke to one of the sailors helping his comrades off the cutter and he told me to explain to the officer at the top of the stairs, and he would sort me out, no problem. So up I went.

At the top of the stairs stood a goliath of a man – the bosun – who was checking in everyone from their ID cards, then he came to me.

"Where is your ID, sailor?" he bellowed in my direction.

"I do not belong..." was as far as I got, before I was pounced upon by a group of burly MPs, who did not want to just cuddle me! I think they knew from my accent that I should not have been there and therefore I must have been a terrorist or, worse still, a spy! I was quickly bundled away to a small, dark room where I was manacled hand and foot to the bulkhead, with only two armed guards for company.

After what seemed an eternity, a gang of people appeared in the doorway, led by the bosun, who told me to stand to attention in the presence of an officer. I would willingly have obeyed had it not been for the manacles being designed for either a four-year-old or a very small dwarf! Nevertheless, I raised myself as high as I could, and opened my mouth to speak. Not only did nothing come out, but my silence was shouted down by my bosun friend.

"Speak when you are spoken to and not before!" he shouted. Fatal mistake, I laughed. I think it was an act of panic rather than happiness... or maybe the fact that I had just realised whom this guy reminded me of, it was BLUTO in the Popeye cartoons! Two huge hands came from nowhere to roughly gag me, my nose was also covered making breathing difficult and I began to feel my head spinning and I think I actually may have passed out. However, I soon recovered as a bowl of ice cold water hit my face.

"Is it true that you are a cook from the British ship?" rasped a question from one of the silhouettes in front of me (the light was behind my tormentors making it impossible to see the features of anyone).

"Yes, sir," I stammered.

"How did you manage to get onto my ship?" came the reply.

"I was with one of your crewmen in a downtown bar, when we were threatened by locals, which prevented us from leaving and so when your shore patrol arrived, we thought it was a good way out for both of us. I had no intention of coming aboard your ship. Indeed, I thought I could get a lift to the docks where I could set off to join my ship.

Unfortunately, I was pushed onto your cutty before I could extricate myself from your guys and here I am," I blurted out, hardly daring to stop for breath.

"What was the name of my sailor?" demanded the voice.

"Gene something, "was my feeble reply.

"Bosun, do we know this man?" asked the voice.

"Yes, sir, I believe he is waiting outside," replied the bosun.

"Well don't just stand there get him in here!" shouted the voice.

To my great relieve, the bosun marched in someone and as soon as he spoke I recognised it was my new friend Gene, who promptly backed my version of what had happened earlier in the evening.

"Right, arrange to get someone who can vouch for this guy, over from the Mauritania.

Once they have identified him, release him to their custody. I am going to bed," and with that the three main silhouettes turned and disappeared out the door.

I did not for one moment think they would use the ship to ship telephone to wake my Captain (after all, it was now well after two o'clock in the morning), who promptly had the head chef woken and sent over to the Wasp, together with our Staff Captain (yes he was woken up as well) and our bosun, to collect one of his "lost lambs". An hour later they were shown into my cell, a light was put on, and someone said, "Yes, that's him." Just as quickly as I was manacled, I was released and marched off the ship, and I did not even have time to have a look around!

Upon our return to the Mauritania, after a totally silent trip, with everyone merely scowling at me, I was told I was on Captain's Report at 1000 hours next morning and sure enough at 0945 hours the bosun appeared in the kitchen to escort me up to the Captain, which was just as well because I did not have a clue where to find him on my own.

Thankfully, it was the Staff Captain that I saw that morning and when I explained what had happened, I am certain that I saw him smile to himself. However, he did fine me two weeks' salary (normally the standard fine was one month's salary), so I think I got off lightly, even if I still do not understand what I had done wrong.

A few nights later I had the opportunity to meet up with Gene and thank him for his help, but this time I went with several other crewmen for company. It was at this meeting that I discovered who my "tormentor" actually was and it turned out to be the Vice Admiral of the whole Seventh Fleet, one of the most important people in the whole of the American Navy. So close a bond had developed between Gene and I that I even went on to meet up with his folks in Trenton, New Jersey, when I next went to the States, particularly as he did not have the chance to go home as his tour of duty lasted for six months without home leave.

CHAPTER SEVEN

My new job was quite exciting as it allowed me to further develop both my management and my organisational skills. I was now personally responsible for a team of eight chefs and for ensuring sufficient food was prepared to cater for all the needs of our passengers, which included ordering the raw food to cover all the menu choices, which was relatively straight forward. The more problematical aspect of this job, was to read the next day's menus and to pick out all the items that my team had to prepare for the main part of the kitchens, particularly cooked garnishes or the preparation of raw meat ready for others to cook e.g. the bread crumbing of raw lamb cutlets ready for shallow frying by the sauce corner. Thankfully, I made very few mistakes.

As I said earlier, I quickly became conversant with my new home port of Naples and its social hotspots, especially when we had the best part of almost two free days there every two weeks. Unlike when I was on the Queen Mary, I did not now have the comfort and luxury of spending all my time off duty with my soul mates (the gang of student cooks who worked and played together). I was virtually on my own now, and it would have been difficult to socialise with the colleagues that I had to manage at work. However, there were a couple of other junior managers with whom I struck up a friendship and we would often spend our off duty time together, not flying off to romantic places, but hiring scooters for the day which allowed us to go off exploring Southern Italy. We particularly liked to go to Rome, as it both had places of interest and a decent night life. The one problem with Italian hire scooters in the early sixties, was that the rear seat of these vehicles was designed to accommodate young ladies; in other words, they were adapted to be ridden side saddle only!

On the surface of it, this would not appear to be significant and those of us who had licences and therefore did the driving soon adapted to the difference in weight distribution. The main problem occurred once we arrived in Rome, because the roads in this city tended to be cobbled and it was not unusual for the drivers to occasionally lose their passengers. Yes, they would literally be bounced off of the rear seat and be deposited on the road! God knows how the Italian women remained on these bikes, or maybe they did not mind embracing their driver and holding on for dear life! Perhaps then, it comes as no surprise that we normally hired a bike each.

We really enjoyed our days out; firstly, there was the beautiful scenery as we made our way north, a journey that took less than a couple of hours. Once in Rome (famously built upon seven hills), we were fortunate enough to have marvelled at the sites, such asThe Colosseum, the largest amphitheatre ever built by the Roman Empire, seating some 60,000 spectators, who regularly gathered to watch the Gladiators.

Then there were the modern versions – the football stadiums of FC Roma and Lazio, The Pantheon, a temple built during Hadrian's rule in 126AD, yet since the 7th century, it has been used as a Roman Catholic Church; The Basilica St John Lateran, the imposing Cathedral of Rome, and we even went to the Vatican (although we never saw the Pope!); The beautiful Trevi Fountain, which was over 85 feet high and some 65 feet wide; The Catacombs, the underground cemeteries dug by all religions to bury their dead; The Olympic Stadium, used for the 1960 Games.

Then there were the Parliament Buildings, City Hall, the various parks, museums, the Arch of Constantine... the list goes on and on and this is not a travel or tourism book.

It was not until later life that we realised just how lucky we were to have had these opportunities.

Rome was a beautiful city, made even better by the fact that we were perfectly safe to wander around both day and night, unlike Naples, where we constantly felt we were at risk of attack.

God! I cannot believe I have been extolling the cultural virtues of a city rather than ranting over its nightclubs and bars. I must have been getting old! Or maybe I was maturing – at last.

The rest of the time we enjoyed nothing better than to soak up the hot Mediterranean sun, by sitting in one of the many pavement cafes and watch the beautiful and stylish women shimmy past Then in the evenings we would go to one of the many bars. I am ashamed to say that in those days, we did drink and drive, although to be fair, there was very little traffic around, compared with today. Then after a meal (one did not eat until after nine o'clock) we would wend our way back to the ship; thankfully, there were not many police about at that time of night either, as I think we may occasionally have exceeded the speed limit! Well, they measured distances in funny things called kilometres which no one understood, and still do not.

My new ship, the steam ship Mauretania, was built by Cammell Laird in Birkenhead for the newly formed Cunard/White Star Line and she was the largest ship built in England up until that time, including the ill-fated Titanic. She weighed 35,739 tonnes, was 772 feet long, 89 feet wide and had a top speed of 23 knots. She was built to replace her namesake, which had been retired in 1935 and to substitute for the Queen Mary and Queen Elizabeth during their annual refits. She was launched on the July 28th 1938, making her maiden voyage on June 17th 1939, sailing between Liverpool and New York.

After two such trips she was moved to the London/ New York run, becoming the largest ship ever to navigate the River Thames.

In December 1939, during World War II, she was commandeered by the government as a troop ship. She was duly painted battleship grey and fitted with two six-inch guns together with other small arms weaponry, she sailed over 540,000 miles and carried over 350,000 troops, accommodating up to 2,000 troops at a time.

After the War in 1946, and having assisted in repatriating troops, she was returned to Cunard, where she had her first major service and refit in seven years. This work included the installation of the revolutionary luxury of air conditioning and her repainting in the company's famous colours of red, white and black.

On April 26th 1947, she recommenced her trips to New York, but Southampton became her home port, this time. In the winter of that year, she first started cruising from New York to the West Indies and then around the Caribbean. She continued this pattern of trans-Atlantic trips in the summer and cruising in the winter, until 1962 (although she commenced her round the world cruises in 1958) when she underwent a major remodelling and refurbishment of her accommodation, which gave her a capacity for 406 passengers in first class, 364 in cabin class and 357 in tourist, giving her a total capacity of 1,127 passengers. It was during this refurbishment that she was first painted the famous cruising green colour, which she retained until her last voyage which commenced on November 10th 1965, after which , she was scrapped.

There were two spooky coincidences, namely both ships that I sailed in were scrapped soon after my leaving them and Captain "Treasure" Jones was her master on her last trip, just as he was the master of the Queen Mary on her final voyage!

My transfer coincided to her change of itinerary to the Mediterranean cruises, then on to New York. These trips went from Naples to Nice, where she docked for approximately Twenty-four hours, and then onto Monaco where she docked for thirty-six hours and finally she crossed the Atlantic to New York. Each crew member's contract lasted for ten weeks, then we had two weeks' leave back in the UK (we were flown by a charter airline between the UK and Naples; these flights replaced their gorgeous female trolley dollies with an all-male crew for some reason?).

It was during my first leave – and as it turned out, my only leave from this ship – that I finally said farewell to my beautiful scooter. For the first couple of days at home I found that all but one of my mates were working and so naturally I went round to see him; big mistake, while I was away he had become a "motorbike scrambling nut" (cross country riding over the worst terrain possible). So Mike and I decided to go up onto the South Downs for some practice; well I thought he would practice and I would watch! Wrong again. Once on the Downs, he showed me the route the riders usually followed, then he rode slowly round the course, showing me how to take the course and where to jump and where to open up the engine etc.

Then, to my surprise, he invited me to have a go, so I got off my bike and started to walk towards his bike.

"Where are you going?" he asked.

"I thought you said I could have a go?" I replied.

"Yes, but I meant on your scooter," he said.

"With its small wheels, it will never get round this course," I said.

"Several club members have scooters... it will be fine," he said reassuringly.

Stupidly, I believed him and set off round the course. I hit every bump full on, and went through the deepest part of every puddle and got stuck in the narrowest ruts going; after all, my tyres were wider than those on a scrambling bike. Needless to say, I came off several times before I limped back over the imaginary finishing line. Nonetheless, I really enjoyed it in a funny sort of way.

"You were not watching me earlier, were you?" Mike asked. "If you were, you totally ignored the tips I was giving you as I rode round. Let me show you again. This time look at my line round the course and watch for when I accelerate."

"But my bike is back heavy and so I cannot jump the same way as you can," I said feebly.

"True, but you can still use the weight to your advantage. Why not follow me round, not too close so you can see what I am doing. It will help you think ahead, as well," Mike suggested.

So off we set. It was much better following ten yards behind him, because I could no longer watch the ground under my tyres, I had to look ahead to see what Mike was doing and in doing so, I anticipated the ground. It really worked, and I was much more fluent second time round. After four circuits, I actually was quite good – even by Mike's standards. Naturally, he was not happy about this and so he duly challenged me to a two lap race. I started well, but his superior bike, designed for this purpose, soon told; well, I think it was when I felt his wheel hit my helmet as he literally OVER took me. Yes, he found a suitable hill to enable him to jump high into the air and his jump took him right over my head and he landed in front of me. After that I only saw him disappearing in the distance. But at least he did not lap me! Well we only did two laps.

After that we went home and I remember it took absolutely ages to clean my bike after that, which put me right off doing that again, which was just as well as it rained for the next couple of days and so it was quite easy to reject his offer for a return race.

Also, if the truth be known, I was fed up getting soaked every time it rained and the final straw came one day when I had forgotten to put my waterproofs into my panier, the heavens opened and drenched me in minutes. But the gods were not satisfied with this and they added insult to injury by tipping me off my scooter as I went round a bend, depositing me in the deepest puddle I had ever seen. OK I exaggerate, but it certainly was the deepest puddle I had ever ended up in, that is for sure! I could almost swim in it.

My misfortunes did not end here, as my bike then refused to restart, forcing me to temporarily abandon it and begin my long ,wet trek home. You can imagine the strange looks I got from passersby; a guy soaked to the skin, with copious amounts of mud and grime dripping off him, for no obvious reason or cause. However, all was not lost, because on my way home I passed a second-hand car showroom which featured the most beautiful Bubble Car I had ever seen – a Bubble Car was the original version of today's Smart Car.

But hey, there was no way that I could go into the showroom in the dishevelled state I found myself in and so I literally ran the rest of the way home for a bath (showers were nonexistent in most average houses in those days). Having tidied myself up, it suddenly dawned upon me that I did not have my scooter, which equally needed a good tidy up and so I had to change, yet again, into clothes which were more suitable for a salvage job.

Luckily the rain had finished and it was much easier getting back to my scooter in the dry. It was only then that I realised that I had not actually examined my vehicle for damage; all I knew was that it would not start after I came off it on a corner and that I could have left behind a mangled mess.

Imagine my relief when I arrived to find that the damage was purely superficial and would probably come off with a little elbow grease; better still, it started first time and I was able to ride it home without any more trouble. You are all thinking that I was very lucky to find my scooter where I left it, but in those days, people were actually more honest and it was very unusual to have your vehicle stolen, irrespective of type. A couple of hours of spit and polish and I was ready to speak to the showroom manager about a deal.

Upon arrival at the showroom I was delighted to find the Bubble Car still there; it was a Heinkel, made in Germany by the famous aircraft company who were banned from aircraft production after the War and so turned their hand to scooters and "micro cars".

The name of bubble car came, in the main, from its bubble shape, although the Messerschmitt resembled the canopy from the famous aircraft of the same name – the whole top lifted up on hinges for people to get into it – and the two occupants sat in tandem one behind the other.

The car I had come to see was bright red, and the whole front opened up on hinges to form the door; inside there were two seats side by side with a luggage rack to the rear and unlike similar cars on the market, when you opened the door, the steering wheel did not move with the door. It had four forward gears, plus a reverse, which I had to have blocked off because I was only licensed to drive motor bikes and scooters.

Bubble Cars had three wheels, normally two at the front and one at the rear. The engine size was somewhere between 174ccs and 210ccs. It was extremely fuel efficient, almost identical to the scooters, and with a top speed somewhere approaching 60 miles an hour, which was very fast for those days.

Anyway, I parked up my bike and tried to nonchalantly walk into the showroom, be cool, do not appear too keen, have a look around before showing any interest in the

Bubble Car... these were all the thoughts coursing through my mind. Suddenly, there was a voice behind me,

"Can I help you, sir?" asked a tall, gaunt looking man, dressed in a grey striped suit.

"Not at the moment," I replied.

"Was sir looking for anything in particular?" he persisted.

I did not know what to say, after all this was the first time I had set foot in a car showroom on my own. *What do you say?* When should you show interest in the vehicle you came into buy?

"Can I just have a look around?" I whimpered feebly.

"Not a problem ,sir," he replied, but he continued to hover around, which unsettled me even more and so I decided it was time to *see* the bubble car. I slowly walked over to this beautiful red shiny vehicle and meandered around it, pretending that I knew what I was looking at. My heart was in my mouth with excitement, but at the same time I could feel it pounding in my chest, as I raised my hand and took hold of the door handle for the first time. I heard the door click open, despite the noise my heart was making and slowly I felt it start to open... wonderful... incredible... heavenly!

Did this old geezer realise what was going on? Surely he could hear my heart pounding?

If he did, it did not show on his face; in fact, nothing showed upon his face, it was emotionless, even his eyes looked like a cod which had been dead for three days. Now was the time, so I climbed in and sat down for the first time, thinking all my Christmases had come at once. It was perfect.

"How much is this?" I stammered.

"It is three hundred pounds," he answered.

"Is there any possibility of part exchange?" I boldly asked.

"It depends upon what you want to exchange," he responded.

"I have a scooter; it's outside if you want to have a look?" I said enthusiastically.

"OK then let's have a look," and we went out to view my bike. He examined it, silently but thoroughly. "Can we test drive it?" he asked eventually.

"Only if I can test the bubble car?" I negotiated.

We went back inside and exchanged keys, his mechanic driving off on my bike and the salesman and I, set off in the bubble car. It was not a real test as I was only allowed to drive around the quiet block, during which, we never met any another vehicle on the road, not even a cat! When we got back, the mechanic was waiting for us and he and his boss quickly fell into a furtive conversation.

"Yes, I might be interested, if the price is right. But I need to make a couple of phone calls first to get a value on your bike though," he said. With that he disappeared into his office to make the said calls.

When he reappeared he came up with a purchase price for my scooter, which I found to be too low and I told him so. To be fair, after a short period of haggling, he did increase his offer to an acceptable level, which he again increased, when he heard I needed some Hire Purchase Finance for the purchase of the Bubble Car. At this point, I was able to strike a deal with Mr Goodham (the tall gaunt man who turned out to be the owner of the showroom), who accepted my bike in part exchange against the Bubble Car, with the outstanding balance being paid off on the "drip" (Hire Purchase). And all that remained before I could proudly leave the showroom with my new car, was for one of my parents to act as guarantor for this transaction. Oh! Just one small problem, they did not even know that I was even thinking about changing vehicles, never mind being about to complete the transaction.

No problem, time for the old charm offensive on Mum; you know how it goes…

"Hi, Mum, you know how I keep coming off my bike, and I keep getting soaked every time it rains. Not to mention how I need much more protection on my trips to Southampton. Well, I think I have found an answer…"

(I did not of course mention the truth about my having to put my girlfriend on the bus and then having to follow the bus and meet her at the other end of her journey, all because her hooped skirt, and her modesty, would not allow her to sit behind me with legs astride my bike! Not to mention how uncomfortable it felt having a male back seat passenger cuddling you when you gave them a lift! Which became even more embarrassing every time you had to break hard and suddenly, as it often caused them to slide forward and almost rape you!

Luckily, Mum fell for it; sorry, I mean ,she agreed to act as my guarantor, and she duly accompanied me to the showroom, there and then, and before the day was out, I became the proud owner of a Bubble Car. Mum was my very first passenger, but I do not remember her hair being quite that grey before I gave her a lift home or was it just the sunlight catching her hair as she got out! Strange that!

It is incredible how popular one becomes, when one is the first in one's circle to own a *car* of any description. Everyone wants you to give them a quick lift as they appear to have missed their last bus (even though it was only ten o'clock), or "sorry, I appear to have spent my bus fare…" or, "I could have sworn I put it in a separate pocket" or best of all, "someone must have picked my pockets". How can you say no to such ingenuity, especially when the request comes from a gorgeous young female! Especially if your own girlfriend was not about! Thankfully the novelty soon wore off and I saved a fortune on petrol as the only journeys I made from then onwards were the ones which I wanted to make.

CHAPTER EIGHT

The worst place to work, in any professional kitchen, is the Roast Corner, not only because it is normally in the physical centre of the kitchen, but also because it generates an enormous amount of heat in the course of its normal work through the equipment it used. Naturally, this heat caused everyone who worked in this area to sweat profusely, so much so that all these staff were required to have salt tablets twice a day, which were supervised by the ship's doctor in person, which showed how important these tablets were to the staff.

For those of you who are not familiar with the organisation of a professional kitchen, the Roast Corner is responsible for all forms of roasting, deep frying (including all varieties of chips) and shallow frying (including the eggs at breakfast). The establishments of Corners were designed both to equalise the workload and to obviate the need to duplicate expensive and space consuming equipment.

As you would expect, their work started first thing in the morning with breakfast, when they would fry up to four long hundreds of eggs (eggs were originally sold by the wholesale unit of one hundred, but because an average of one in five were bad, an extra twenty eggs were included free per hundred in order to comply with the Laws of the Land relevant at that time). Ergo, the long hundred, which is still being used as the wholesale unit for eggs, today. This is also true of bread; the bakers dozen is thirteen loaves which ensures that the customer got the full weight measure they had paid for – this is still a familiar term used today.

The frying pans used to fry the eggs, held a dozen eggs at a time and were used exclusively for this purpose to ensure they never stuck. Normally, one chef was able to meet the demand for freshly fried eggs, however, if he got "up the wall" (a technical term for someone who was under pressure), a second person would move in to assist until the rush was over.

By controlling the temperature of the pans, it was common practice for the first eggs to be ready by the time you had finished cracking the twelfth egg, that is assuming that everyone wanted their eggs sunny side up, variations like over easy or hard yolks caused temporary mayhem for the poor fryer! Once the eggs were cooked they were lifted out onto a tray and a second person, who was on service, took them to the hotplate and served them to the waiters. If ever you dropped an egg on the deck, there was no point in trying to pick it up, as it would cook on contact with the floor, further evidence of how hot it was in this part of the kitchen.

To make the service more efficient, all breakfast items served in the first-class dining room, were silver serviced – not the easiest of tasks for the waiters, but possible if you used two fish knives to serve fried eggs. This took the pressure off of the kitchen but it made breakfast the worst meal of the day for the waiting staff, as they had fruit juices, tea/coffee, bread, rolls and toasts, to serve too, and these items came from the stillroom and not the kitchen, therefore, team work amongst the waiters was essential if they were to provide a successful breakfast.

But life was not without some pluses for the Roast Corner, as they were also the only staff on the whole ship, to be legally given a daily allowance of beer to replace the liquids lost through their profuse sweating. What a hardship! Furthermore, they were the only chefs who did not have to wear the thick heavily starched chef's jackets, and as a consequence, they mostly wore T-shirts, which they changed every hour or so.

Nevertheless, they still had to go and collect their beer though, using the tokens given to them for payment; well, that is not strictly true, as they sent their kitchen porter to collect each round!

The chef de partie in charge of this area of work, was known as Yogi, as he physically resembled the well-known television character, popular at that time, namely, tall and portly with a somewhat gormless expression permanently on his face (although he never wore a pork pie hat, as far as I can remember). When he spoke, it was rather slow and deliberate, and his voice was deeper than usual, all of which gave the erroneous impression that he might be at least one sandwich short of a picnic, which in actual fact, was very far from the truth as he was quite intelligent and very well read, which he underlined every time there was a quiz on the ship. I have never known anyone to become so instantly popular, as everyone else literately fought one another to get him on their quiz team! He won the quiz virtually single handedly, and the winners always benefited from their share of quite a valuable cash prize.

During working hours, Yogi was a consummate professional; he worked hard and expected the same from his team and it was very unusual for him to behave in a manner unbecoming to a senior rating. However, that is not to say that he never behaved in a manner unbecoming a chef de partie (chef in charge of a section of the kitchen).

Occasionally, he would get bored and revert to practical jokes on colleagues. His party piece was, just before service, placing a raw turkey neck in the fly of his chef's trousers, leaving the vast majority sticking out, although it would be hidden underneath his apron. When the female cabin maids came to collect their luncheon, he would wait for a new face to appear in front of him, on the other side of the hotplate, and then in the blink of an eye he would lift his apron, grab hold of the turkey neck and scream (as if in pain) something along the lines of: "I cannot stand it anymore... this damn dose of the clap is driving me mad!" and with that he would place the neck onto the chopping board in front of him and with his large chopping knife, he would cut it cleanly in half. As the whole operation took less than two seconds, more than one young lady thought they just witnessed him cutting off his manhood and would promptly faint!

As you can well imagine, this was an extremely rare occurrence, it had to be, to maximise its impact upon the unsuspecting victim, when he did repeat the "amputation". Also, by allowing ample time between performances, people would have forgotten what they had just witnessed and consequently, would have no reason to warn future potential victims about the possibility of a repeat performance. Furthermore, it was somewhat difficult to obtain a raw turkey neck without people asking questions.

In the evenings, after he had finished work, Yogi loved to spend his time in the Pig where he would heavily imbibe in the amber nectar and it was not unusual for him having to be helped back to his cabin and into his bunk; indeed, he was often found sleeping in his wardrobe because he was so drunk that he kept falling out of his bunk! On another occasion, he failed to turn to, for duty in the morning, consequently, his deputy, on realising he was absent and not just late, sent a kitchen porter down to his cabin, to wake him up. Unfortunately, he was unable to rouse the unconscious Yogi and so he returned to the kitchen empty handed. The deputy, fearful of the repercussions that would arise should the head chef discover the absence, went down himself to rouse the sleeping beauty.

He also failed to revive the sleeping giant and sought the help of the glory hole steward, who suggested they poured cold water over Yogi to wake him up. Accordingly, when the steward went to get some water, the desperate deputy placed his cigarette lighter under the water sprinkler over Yogi's bunk, little realising that this would set off the sprinklers in the whole of this section and worse still, it set off the fire alarm throughout the whole ship!

Upon hearing the fire alarm, everyone, from passengers to crew, immediately made their way, as quickly as they could, to their allocated lifeboat stations, complete with their lifejackets and all ready to be loaded into the lifeboats, should the order to abandon ship be given. Today was no exception; yes, everyone went to their lifeboat stations!

Meanwhile, the specialist firefighting team, complete with breathing apparatus, rushed to their designated manning point, to await redirection to that area of the ship which was identified as being the danger area, where they would begin their meticulous search of each cabin, for the fire and its source. In other words, there was total pandemonium!

At the same time, below deck in Yogi's cabin, the cold water from the overhead sprinklers had had the desired effect; in other words, it woke Yogi, who not only woke up, but in the ensuing chaos, had made his way up to the kitchen to start work, despite being soaking wet though! I do not think he even realised he was the only person working in the whole of the kitchen.

The best story ever to do the rounds about Yogi, involved his car, a prized and much loved Austin Seven, although I always had great difficulties imagining him squashing his large frame into such a small car. Anyway, so the story goes, he was driving back to the ship one day, when a car wheel suddenly overtook him – no it was not attached to any car, van or lorry! He was quoted as saying: "Some stupid bastard has just lost their wheel!"

Anyhow, he thought no more about it and continued on his way back to the ship. Then, when he got out, his whole car tipped over onto one side, away from him. Yes, it was his own front nearside wheel, which had come off and rolled down the street, ahead of him, but because of his weight and size, he still balanced the car. That is until he got out of it!

As a result of this incident, his whole front axle was ruined, and because of its age, he could not find a replacement and his beloved car had to be consigned to history and the scrap yard.

This was my first trip in my newly promoted role, as a chef de partie and an integral part of my new responsibilities was, to skipper lifeboat 13, should the need arise. This had not really bothered me because in spite of the Board of Trade requirement for lifeboats to be lowered into the sea and the engines tested, this normally happened when the ship was in port, so the process could be witnessed by representatives from the Board, which in turn, allowed the lifeboats to be certified as being seaworthy. However, we always tied up alongside with odd numbered lifeboats next to the quayside making it impossible for my boat ever to be lowered!

But this was not my lucky day. As the ship was making excellent progress and as the ship had stopped anyway, because of the emergency, the Captain decided to seize the moment and lower two randomly chosen lifeboats... yes, you guessed it, number 13 was one of the chosen ones, subsequently, all one hundred and ten people, allotted to lifeboat 13 were loaded up and gently lowered into the sea.

The normal procedure was for the engineers, allocated to that lifeboat, to start the engine and then to sail round the ship before being hoisted back up, all of which should have taken about forty minutes in total. But as I said previously, this was not my day because my engineers failed to get the engine to start and some idiot cast us off from the davits, prior to being given the order to disengage, which left us drifting helplessly in mid Atlantic! This left me with no choice – besides panicking – except to give the order to break out the oars and to row back to the ship; well, it was only about fifty yards. OK, it was against the current, but I did have thirty crew to row.

Unfortunately, it took almost an hour to reach the ship and that was thanks to several of the passengers kindly helping to row, probably because they were frightened of being abandoned by the mother ship. Nevertheless, we finally managed to get alongside and the deckhand responsible for getting us connected to the ship, used his pole to hook the davit and pull us in, just as a wave hit the side of the ship and pushed us away from the ship, leaving the deckhand clinging onto the davit, some three feet above the sea!

Luckily, we were able to manoeuvre the boat back alongside to pick up the poor matelot before he fell into the sea. More importantly, our second attempt to attach to the davits was successful and in no time we were hoisted back up onto the boat deck, where we were greeted by an ovation of clapping and cheering from the passengers who had stayed behind to watch the fun. Only an hour later than planned!

It goes without saying that the Captain was not as happy and next morning I was marched in to meet him... this was not a social visit of course, but to explain my gross incompetence on the previous day. The result of which was that I was logged (fined) a month's pay and ordered to undergo a course on lifeboat management when I was next in dock in Southampton. (Apparently, this is still recorded in the ship's log today, where ever it may be, as are all other disciplinary punishments handed out by the Captain.)

Meanwhile, the gallant firefighters having failed to find any sign of a fire, recommended that the all clear be sounded. However, the ship's bosun who was in charge of the firefighters, just happened to see Yogi making his way back to his cabin, still soaking wet, which aroused his suspicions. Yogi managed to talk his way out of an embarrassing situation by claiming he was in his cabin to collect another pack of cigarettes (despite being a non-smoker) when the sprinkler system went off. As no one could disprove his story and no one was prepared to give evidence against him, he managed to get away with it – as did his deputy – making me the only crewman to be punished, despite my not having been involved or having any responsibility for causing the problems!

Needless to say, it cost Yogi and his deputy a huge bar bill, which ensured the silence of all the crew members whose belongings had been ruined by the sprinklers and it was not long before the sheer stupidity of the whole episode became a huge joke, which was even enjoyed by those members of the crew who lost possessions. Even so, despite the huge number of people who knew the truth about what actually happened, the ship's formal investigation never did discover the truth and the eventual conclusion was that there had been a system failure. This outcome delighted all of the crew who lived in the water soaked section, because this decision allowed them all, including Yogi and his deputy, to claim for all their possessions which were ruined by the water, from the company!

Naturally, no one made any fictitious claims nor claimed for anything which had not been damaged!

One evening, not long after the infamous "Episode of the Phantom Sprinkler", the ship carried a young film starlet, who had made her name from the nightie she wore in her maiden film. Although she was now rich, and famous as a sex symbol, her film company had never educated her in how to behave in public, especially in the refinements of dining. Consequently, she embarrassed herself many times on that crossing, especially when she ordered caviar for the first time and having tasted it, sent it back because it tasted "salty and fishy".

On another occasion, I was booked by her station waiter, one evening, to take my solid silver carving trolley, containing a whole untouched roast sirloin of beef, over to Miss X.

When I asked how she liked her beef (well done would have been cut from the outside of the joint; a medium portion would have been cut from just inside either end and if the customer wanted a rare portion, it would have been cut from the middle of the joint), to my total surprise, she said she wanted a slice from right across the whole length of the joint. Despite being star struck, not to mention being dazzled by her very revealing cleavage (remember I was standing up and she was seated below me, which may have enhanced the view, not that I looked you understand), I tried to explain that this was not possible as it would spoil the joint for other customers. Unfortunately, she became insistent and irritated, once again, the customer is always right and so I had to concede. I duly sliced a piece from the two foot length of beef which I duly concertina folded onto a plate and served to Miss X, together with two individual Yorkshire Puddings!

There was nothing else I could do but to take the remains of the mutilated joint back out to the kitchen and to ask Yogi for a replacement. He naturally went ballistic, and had to be physically restrained as he fully intended to go into the restaurant and give this young lady a piece of his mind. So noisy was his outburst that it attracted the attention of the head chef, who promptly came over to see what the fuss was all about and to my amazement he also went spare, throwing the remainder of the sinned against sirloin across the kitchen. Before anyone knew what was happening, the chef disappeared into the restaurant, fully intent on sorting out Miss X. He duly returned some five minutes later, telling everyone what a gorgeous young lady Miss X was and held up an autographed photograph, complete with the imprint of her lips where she had kissed the photograph. He was clearly in love, despite being well over sixty years of age, and we all know love is blind and his cherished photograph took pride of place in his office... he even had it framed when we reached port. For the rest of that trip, he insisted on dealing with Miss X's order personally to ensure everything was perfect; he even accompanied her main course out into the restaurant every evening!

As for Yogi, he never did forgive her for ruining one of his precious joints of beef, bearing in mind the sirloin was the only joint ever to be knighted and Yogi always treated it like royalty and to rub salt into his wounds, he did not even get an autographed photograph. I believe to this day, he has never seen one of her films, which must have clearly wreaked havoc upon her bank account! Although come to think of it Yogi never went to the cinema anyway, probably because no cinema ever served beer while you watched the film, not even in the sixties and he would never have wasted valuable drinking time!

CHAPTER NINE

One evening in late April, the ship encountered some really rough seas and as a result not many passengers were interested in dinner – for some reason? So, Johnnie allowed some of us to finish work at 2130 hours, a good couple of hours early and I happened to be one of the lucky ones, so I decided to return to my cabin to have a shower and freshen up prior to a couple of drinks in the Pig. Upon opening my cabin door, I was greeted by the sight of a naked bum, gyrating on my bunk!

"What the hell's going on?" I found myself whispering, for some obscure reason.

"Sorry. Can you go to the Pig, I'll pay for the drinks and I'll join you there in a couple of shortly..." I instantly recognised the voice of my new cabin mate, Roland. Although I have to admit, I did not immediately recognise the bum! Without thinking, I automatically closed the door and obediently disappeared off to the Pig, although I do remember wondering whose bum it was I had seen and why was it in my bunk?

Half an hour later, Roland joined me, but I was more interested in his "companion" whom I saw scuttling off as quickly as possible, especially as they were dressed in a chef's uniform. Surely, he was not a homosexual!

"You haven't started 'batting for the other side' have you?" I asked. I was more worried about my own safety (after all we did share the same room and his bunk was ABOVE mine).

"Don't be crazy!" came the incredulous retort. "Look, I am really sorry, but I thought we had another hour at least before you would finish work," he blurted out, "and we would have finished and been well away!"

"Look, I think you had better start at the beginning," I said.

"OK, but first let me get another round in and then I will explain," and off he went to get the drinks.

"Two weeks ago, while we were in Southampton, I was walking back to the ship, when I saw Connie, a Purserette who is one of our bloods, struggling with two large heavy, awkward shaped bags. So I offered to help her back to the ship. Naturally, we spoke as we walked along. Anyway, to cut a long story short, when we reached the ship, she asked me if I fancied a 'bit of fun'. Next thing I knew she was smuggling me into one of the cabins she looked after while at sea. Well, we started snogging and as you can imagine, one thing led to another."

"Good God!" I interrupted. "Do you mean you shagged the arse off her? She is old enough to be your mother!" I guessed Connie was in her early forties, but to be fair she was in very good condition considering how old she was. We were still only nineteen, and anyone in their forties was an ancient! "You total pervert," I sneered.

"Look, you are only jealous as you did not get the chance. Anyhow, she has taught me a hell of a lot already. Haven't you noticed her arse. It is so small and tight, perfectly formed. When she walks, it is like watching the two ferrets fighting in a sack, but these two are seriously overactive! When I am on top of her, there is nothing better than to grab hold of her arse and pull her towards me. Mind once she gets going, I need something to hold on to!" Roland said.

"What do you mean?" I asked eagerly.

"Well, as I was saying, there we were in this locked passenger cabin, snogging away, when she broke off and slowly sank to her knees and started to undo my flies. She then dropped both my trousers and my jocks (his word for underpants) and started to run her tongue around my balls."

"You great big lying bastard. In your dreams!" I interjected.

"No. Straight up! Before I knew what was going on she started to run her tongue up and down my dick, I even felt it flicking under my helmet! Then all of a sudden it was in her mouth and she began to gently suck it! I have never felt anything like it in my life. As you can imagine, it was not long before I 'shot my load', straight into her mouth! I could not believe it, the dirty cow actually swallowed it!" he explained.

"I have heard the older guys brag about this," I said. "You are describing a blow job, she actually gave you a genuine blow job. God, I never believed that people actually did such things. What happened then? What was it like?" I asked eagerly.

"It was absolutely brilliant," he said. "But unfortunately it did not last long as I got so exited. But it did not end there. She almost ripped off all her clothes right there in front of me, before removing the rest of my clothes and then she pulled me onto the bed. She pushed my head down onto her breasts and told me to gently suck them, which of course I did. I remember running my tongue around her nipples, both of them naturally, and I even felt them harden in response to my caress with my tongue. After a while she gently pushed my head even lower until I was opposite to her 'pussy'. 'Kiss me. Kiss me,' she purred. 'Give me a French kiss,' she pleaded.

"I was only too happy to oblige," he said with a glint in his eye. "She moved her body in response to my tongue, which appeared to increase her pleasure. She pointed out something she called her 'G Spot', and when my tongue touched it, I felt her dribble all down my tongue and into my mouth. If I had had time to think about it, I would probably have thrown up, but no, this was not an unpleasant taste; in fact, I enjoyed it!

"All of a sudden she moaned and grabbed hold of my ears and pulled me even closer to her, making it almost impossible for me to breathe and I felt my mouth filling up with this silky smooth liquid. It was heavenly. The only thing I did not like was the fact that I was pulling pubic hairs out of my teeth for hours afterwards!"

"I cannot believe what you are telling me! What did it taste like? What happened next?" I implored him eagerly. Well, I had never heard anything like it in all my life, certainly not in such detail and not from someone describing their personal and actual experience.

"The nearest thing I can compare this taste to is a lightly seasoned Mousseline Sauce; Well, we were chefs! By this time I was fully aroused again, so I remounted and gave her another good seeing to, so much so that my lower groin bone began to really hurt, which was probably a result of me pushing too hard and too deep! It was absolutely incredible, I have never had a shag like it. Since then we have been at it at every opportunity and she has continued to share her sexual experience and knowledge with me... the best education I have ever had, and, best of all, it was all free!" he said.

"Where have you been doing it? Not always in passenger accommodation surely? If you get caught you will both be for the high jump. Please don't tell me you have been using my bunk all this time! Oh God, how can I get it sterilised? I want a new bunk!" I said.

"No. Last time in New York, we hired a room for the night, and what a night it was! First of all, we had a bath together. Then she taught me how to explore all the sensual places on her body: her toes; her knees; the inside of her wrists; the inside of her thighs; the front of her neck; her ears; the top of her shoulders; the small of her back, and even the cheeks of her arse! The places were endless. I do not even remember half of them."

"Tell me about the positions she has taught you?" I was beginning to sound like a pervert!

"She loves it when I sit astride her and roll her breasts around my dick, but I have to be careful not to get overexcited... she tells me to think of something else – as if! Then, she loves it when I take her from the rear."

"What you actually stick it up her bum?" I gasped in disgust.

"No, you fool, not up the bum; we stand up and I place my dick in her pussy from the rear and at the same time, hold onto both her breasts, to help us keep our balance. It is the same as the doggy position, but standing up."

I nodded knowledgeably, but in reality, I did not have a clue as to what he was actually talking about... we never did things like this on the football or cricket pitch.

"So where else have you had it?" I asked.

"Last time in Southampton, we went to the New Forest in a borrowed car. Well as you can guess we had to stop before we even got there… into the back, even though it was broad daylight, and had sex. We then stopped at a pub for lunch, and by the time we reached the New Forest it was starting to get dark. It was then that Connie had this idea that she wanted sex under the stars, and so we looked for a field and we found and old rug in the car!

"We stripped off and began to enjoy each other. I was on top of her when I experienced a weird sensation around my bum! God, what are you doing to me now? Connie had a quizzical look on her face. 'What do you mean?' she said. I looked around to see a dog licking my naked bum," he said. "I could not believe it, but worst still, I could not move. I froze with fear as I have always been scared of dogs, and this was a big dog. "'There's a dog licking my bum, Connie! What should I do? Connie could not speak; she was too busy laughing! 'Chase it away,' she eventually muttered.

"Are you sure it won't bite me; after all, I am in no position to defend myself. How could I explain my injuries to the hospital," he mused. After all, he was in the middle of full blown sex and a "ménage a trios" was not designed to include a dog, as far as we knew.

"So what did you do?" I asked, while pinching myself so that I did not start laughing.

"I shouted; well, whispered in a serious voice for it to go away. Well I think the dog was more scared than I was and it turned on its hind legs and run off into the dark. It probably went off somewhere to die. After licking my arse, it probably did die!

"Well after that, I certainly was not in the mood, so we got dressed and went back to the ship. After that, things were never the same again and we gradually grew apart and our relationship finished a few days later."

It was quite late and so we turned in. We never had such a detailed conversation about women again, although we continued to brag to each other about our fantasies (we never had time to meet girls with whom we could have a relationship and so most of our bragging was in reality the figment of our over active imagination).

By now, you are probably asking yourself, *how can you remember a conversation which happened over forty years earlier?* The answer is quite easy. This was the first real, adult conversation about sex I had ever had with someone who had actually been doing it, and you do not forget such things, just like your first kiss, I suppose.

As for Roland, I met him a couple of years later and guess what? He had actually turned gay! So much for older women.

CHAPTER TEN

Because of the sheer size of the kitchens and the noise they generated, the only means of communication between the chef's office and the rest of the kitchen staff, was via a tannoy system (the 1930s version of an intercom.) Midway through breakfast one morning, on the way to New York, the head chef was heard to bellow over the tannoy: "Laurence (who was his secretary and personal valet), you lazy B*****d, get your f*****g lazy arse over here (or words similar in sentiment to this)." He screeched this command out several times more and each time he sounded as if he was getting angrier and angrier. As you can imagine, everyone in the kitchen kept their heads down in the hope that he would not come out of his office and vent his anger out upon them.

"Has anyone seen Laurence? For C****t's sake, hasn't anyone seen him? Answer me, even if it is only to say no!" Eventually, he grabbed hold of an unsuspecting passing member of staff.

"Get down to the lazy b****r's room and get him out of his pit at once!" he shrieked.

"Where does he live?" quivered the poor wretch.

"How the hell should I know! Do I look like the f*****g Staff Captain?" replied the chef.

Luckily for him, a friendly face, still fearing the retribution of the "Lord", told the poor wretch, whose name was Andy, where to find the secretary's cabin. Andy was a huge guy, almost 6feet 6inches tall and weighing some 16 stone. Unfortunately, he abused the privilege of being ugly; in fact, he made Shrek look handsome! He was, however, a very naïve guy, with no ambition and was just happy to plod along, which was probably the reason why he was happy to work as a kitchen porter. Despite his lowly position and demeanour, Andy was a likeable young guy and he would quite often join us students when off duty, dependent upon his work rotas of course.

One of his endearing features was that the poor guy could not drink; well, he could and did drink, and he got drunk after two or three pints, which considering his size always appeared somewhat unusual. When he was drunk, which was every time we went out, he was an extremely funny guy, but he was a very lonely guy. He even told us that he had never had a girlfriend, despite the fact that he was 22 years old! So, one evening, we decided to fix him up with a woman, no easy task bearing in mind how quickly he got drunk. Come to think about it that was the best time to fix him up, because when he was sober, he was quite boring and no woman would ever see beyond his looks as his true personality did not surface until he had had a few drinks!

This evening, the four of us linked up in a pub with four young ladies and to our surprise Andy took a shine to one of them. Her name was Roweena, and he spent quite a long time talking to her. They laughed and joked for well over an hour before she got up to go to the loo, and it was then we realised for the first time that she was one of those ladies who had an exceptionally long body but no legs... well of course she had legs, but they were very short! In fact, she was only about five feet tall, but this fact was hidden from us all the time she was sitting down. I can honestly say that she was taller sitting down than she was standing up, if you can understand that!

Roweena, or Ribena as we called her, could not have weighed more than six stone as she was extremely slim (or should I describe her as very thin? OK, she was downright skinny!). Her mousey coloured hair flowed down her back to her waist and it was probably her best feature. Her face was very plain and her buck teeth seemed to dominate her visage; it was obvious that she did not wear make-up of any description, which was most unusual for a young lady in those days. As I said earlier, her legs appeared to be very short, but they were also very thin, what could in all honesty, be best described as true matchsticks!

The odd couple, as we came to know them, hit it off straightaway and that was all that was important to us supporters and it surprised no one when, at the end of the night, they made their excuses and left together, hardly hand in hand as Andy's arms were not that long! We bid them a fond farewell and said we would see them later, whatever that meant. The remainder of the group sat there agog, with their mouths wide open; the boys were amazed because finally, Andy had pulled and the girls were equally astounded as they genuinely thought Ribena was a lesbian, as she had never previously shown any interest in men, and had even refused to dance with any of the guys who had asked her.

Next morning, we all rushed to meet up with Andy to discover how he got on. Imagine our disappointment when he told us that he could not remember anything about the night before, which was not surprising as he seldom remembered anything after a few drinks with us! However, by lunchtime, his memory had returned a little and when we went for a smoke, he confided in me, for some reason. He did remember going back to her flat, and he did remember that they had become "amorous".

"How the hell did you manage that?" I asked without thinking.

"We are all the same size lying down," he replied, with a glint in his eye.

"Are you going to tell me what happened then?" I asked.

"Only if you promise not to tell any of the others," he continued. "When we got to her place, we sat on her sofa (an old-fashioned name for a settee) and she kissed me. Naturally I kissed her back, and one kiss led to another sort of thing. Before I knew what was happening she was ripping my clothes off and so I started to remove hers, but as I have never taken a woman's clothes off before, I really found it very difficult and I am afraid in the end she had to take her own clothes off! All I could do was sit there in my underwear and watch her. Remember, I was pissed at the time and found it difficult to actually focus on anything in particular, in fact her body was a bit of a blur.

"When she was naked, she came over and sat right next to me and then she put my hands upon her breasts. They were nowhere near as big as the breasts I have seen in the men's magazines though; they were more like two fried eggs, well perhaps not even as big as that, in fact if it were not for her nipples, she would not have had any breasts at all!

Anyway, I gently caressed what was there; I think I may even have kissed her nipples. While I was doing this, she removed my underpants and took hold of my willie. I thought it was going to explode as she gently began to stroke it. I have never felt anything like it in all my life.

"The next thing I remember, I found myself pushing into her body; you know what I mean, the hairy part down there," he said, pointing down to his lower anatomy. "It was so difficult to get in and it really hurt me, but I heard her moan and so I continued. I must say I was not really enjoying this experience, it was like rubbing two hairy coconuts around my willie... not that I have ever done that," he added hastily.

"Didn't you have any foreplay?" I asked, trying to sound knowledgeable in such matters.

"What do you mean by foreplay?" Andy asked me.

"You mean you did not play with her pussy until it became moist?" I said. (I remember reading that this was necessary before sex, or something like this, in a magazine.) I just felt that as Andy had asked, I could at least try to be helpful, even though I did not really have a clue about what I was talking about.

"No, I did not play with it first, I just went straight in, that must have been why it was so very dry and painful. Anyway, before I knew it, I had ejaculated. The whole thing could not have lasted more than three minutes! You do not think she is pregnant do you?"

"It only happened last night, she cannot be pregnant yet. Didn't you even wear a rubber?" (that was the street name for a condom) I asked.

"Do you really think that as soon as I realised what was happening, I was going to stop. To get dressed and go down to the nearest pub and buy some rubbers? Yeah, I'm sure," he scoffed. "After ejaculation, I felt so embarrassed that I just got dressed and left."

"Are you going to see her again?" I asked.

"I don't know," he said. "In fact, I cannot even remember what she looks like."

I must admit, I did not keep my promise; in fact, I could not wait to tell the gang that Andy had got laid. From then onwards he became a bit of a hero for us students… after all, he had lost his cherry. That night we took him out to celebrate. I think we told him it was someone's birthday and as our guest at the party, he did not have to pay for any drinks that night (not that it was going to be very expensive subsidising his drinking!).

As the evening went on, we moved onto the club where Andy had struck lucky the night Before, and guess what, Ribena was there! She immediately got up and rushed towards Andy, and when she reached him, she jumped up and kissed him. Once again they ensconced themselves in a corner and continued where they left off, kissing and cuddling. However, before they left that night, Andy made an urgent and unexpected visit to the loo.

Unfortunately, this love story did not last very long. Roweena met the ship upon its next arrival in Southampton and Andy saw her for the first time, and he was sober and it was still daylight. As soon as he got down the gangplank, she rushed up to him and tried to give him a great big kiss, but as Andy did not lean forward, her efforts failed because she could not reach his mouth.

"What the hell are you doing here? We did not arrange to meet," he rasped.

"I thought I would surprise you," she replied. "Did I do wrong?"

Andy was very surprised to see her and obviously embarrassed by her attempted show of affection in front of his mates.

"We need to go somewhere less public where we can talk," he said.

"We could go to my place. There is no one there and we can have some fun," she replied.

Andy was insistent and he took her by the arm and led her off. Later we discovered that they went to the local coffee bar. His response must have been a real shock to poor Ribena and not at all what she was expecting.

"What's wrong, Andy? Have I done something wrong? Are you mad with me?" she Garbled.

"Look," said Andy. "I do not think this is going to work..."

"Why not?" Ribena interrupted.

"Let me finish and everything will become very clear," Andy went on. "As you may have guessed, I am not very experienced with women and had had a few bevies when we first met. I simply was not prepared for what happened that night. This is very difficult for me to explain, and right from the start it has been obvious that you are quite experienced with this sex thing, which I am finding difficult to deal with. Do you understand what I am saying?" he mumbled.

"No, I haven't a clue what you are talking about," she replied nervously.

"Look, it is embarrassing to have you dominate in the bedroom and I cannot deal with it. I want a woman who is my equal. Someone I can learn together with; someone who does not make me feel inferior. God damn it, I do not want a girlfriend who is obviously sexually experienced!" he blurted out.

"Are you dumping me? Please don't! I love you!" she sobbed.

"Sorry, but I cannot handle this… it is best if we leave it and go our separate ways. Sorry!" and with that, he stood up and dashed out the door, leaving behind a heart broken and bewildered woman, sobbing her heart out, but not really understanding just why her heart had just been broken.

We did not see Andy socially for the rest of that leave and indeed he kept himself to himself for the first two days at sea; once we had set sail in a funny sort of way I think he was feeling sorry for himself and needed time to "lick his wounds". But here he was, brought down to the realities of life by a very irate chef, who was demanding that he went down to his cabin and wake up his secretary, wherever he lived on the ship! So frightened was he that he disappeared round the corner as quick as his legs could carry him; he literally seemed to disappeared in a puff of smoke, so quick was his exit. When he eventually found the secretary's cabin, the poor innocent, gently knocked on the door.

Upon receiving no reply, he knocked again, but this time a little louder, and so it continued until he was thumping the door as hard as he could, but still without reply. As you might expect, the row soon attracted the attention of others, particularly the steward for that section.

"What the f**k do you think you are doing?" he bellowed. "You cannot come down here waking up all my boys. Some of these guys work nights you know! Why don't you clear off!"

"The chef wants Laurence up in the kitchen immediately and I cannot get a reply," responded the poor kitchen porter, who by now, was beginning to feel suicidal.

"But I woke him up with a cup of tea, at 0630 hours as usual," said the steward.

"Did you actually speak to him? Then he must have gone back to sleep," said Andy.

"No one could sleep through the row you have made, you pillock," derided the steward.

"There must be something wrong!" It is incredible how quick and perceptive some people get in a possible emergency. With that he grabbed the door handle and threw open the door. "Come on, Laurence, old mate, the old man is going spare!" called the Steward as he walked towards the bunk. As he drew nearer he saw the full cup of tea he had left several hours earlier.

Unfortunately, there was no response from the bunk and so he shook the prone figure in the bunk. He immediately jumped back in horror.

"Good God, I think he is dead," he screamed. "Quickly, go and get the ship's doctor. Tell him to come at once!" he shouted.

"Shouldn't I go and tell the chef what is going on first?" begged the poor porter.

"No! A bloke's life may be at stake here! Forget old misery guts and just get the Doc!"

"Oh God, are you sure he's dead?" asked the porter, as he disappeared out the door.

"Just hurry up!" screamed the steward.

A few minutes later, he reappeared with the Doc in tow.

"Wait outside," said the Doc. "I will sort this out." Within a few minutes, the Doc appeared to announce that Laurence was in fact dead.

They could see over his shoulder that the Doc had covered the corpse with his own blanket. Realising how futile the situation was, poor Andy returned to the kitchen to break the sad news to the impatient chef. As he looked back, he saw the doctor lock the cabin door and walk slowly away in the opposite direction"Where the f*****g hell have you been? Enjoy your f*****g holiday?" shouted the chef upon seeing Andy.

"Chef, I am ever so sorry, but Laurence is dead," whimpered the porter as apologetically as he could manage.

Upon hearing of his secretary's demise, the chef was heard to mumble, "Trust that inconsiderate bastard to die. He could at least have f*****g waited until he woke me up with my morning cup of tea. Where the f*****g hell am I going to find a f*****g replacement in the middle of the f*****g Atlantic? Where is he? Can I see him?"

"I found him in his bunk, in his cabin. I think he died in his sleep. The Doc has locked his room, so I do not think you will be able to get in," said Andy.

The chef promptly turned on his heal and retreated into his office. I was reliably informed that his behaviour was mere bravado and the chef was in fact totally devastated by this death and used this veneer to hide his true emotions; they had in fact worked together for over ten years and had formed quite a strong personal bond. He never did come to terms with the fact that Laurence had died alone. He had no known family; he had never been married, and nor was he a member of the gay fraternity.

He always maintained that his work and the people he worked with, were his family.

People are always asking me, "Why do chefs always swear so much and why are they so temperamental?"

The answers are fairly complicated but I will try to enlighten everyone. I just hope that none of the television celebrity chefs read this, as I am certain they will do more than just swear at me!

As you will have seen from the menus in an earlier chapter, chefs not only require a certain amount of latent artistic ability, but are also "perfectionists", which means they put a lot of undue pressure upon themselves to achieve the self-imposed standards. It goes without saying that it is almost impossible to achieve these standards at all times and consequently their frustrations are viewed as temperament. These self-imposed pressures, are further amplified by the ever-present dangers they work under, some of which are self-evident:

- Burns – obviously when anyone works with hot equipment, naked flames and high temperatures, there is always a real risk of burning oneself.

- Heat – all kitchens get hot, bur commercial kitchens can be extremely hot. As a result it is not uncommon for people to faint from this heat.

- Sharp Equipment – naturally working with knives will always involve a risk of cutting yourself (the worst case scenario being, trying to catch a dropped knife which slips through the fingers – ouch! However, there are other and more serious risks which will not only cut you, but just as easily take a finger or worse off, including meat cleavers (choppers), rotary bowl choppers (a horizontal rotating bowl with vertical scimitar blades), mincing machines, mixers/ blenders, waste disposals etc.

- Spillages – wet floors in a kitchen are ever present and can easily cause people to slip and fall onto hot surfaces or hurt themselves by hitting something on their way down.

- Fires – it is not unusual for frying pans to cause flash fires which can easily cause injury by singeing hair or causing severe burns.

- Time pressures – meal times normally begin at a set time and our customers expect the food to be ready (when was the last time you went into a restaurant and the chef came out and told you he was not ready and asked you to amuse yourself until he was ready?). Consequently, the pressure tends to build in any kitchen, as the service time approaches, particularly if they are behind in their work. This often manifests itself in a slight shortening of tempers; chefs go berserk for no apparent reason and physical fights amongst themselves are not uncommon. Although to be honest, it is more common for a chef to take it out on a waiter (considered parasites who earn tips from the expertise of the chef!), normally by pulling them forward across the hotplate and holding them there! Having said that, we do not hold grudges and are often seen drinking with each other immediately after the service has finished!

The above list is not definitive but merely a sample of the dangers and when you add the human effect of carelessness and lapse in concentration, you are left with a ticking time bomb! It will not come as any surprise to learn that one in every three chefs will have a least one serious injury in their working life... who wants to be a chef!

In short, is it any wonder, that we chefs swear a lot!

A few days later, at eleven o'clock, Laurence was buried on the aft deck, when the secretary was committed to the sea in a ceremony attended by virtually all the catering staff, plus a couple of hundred curious passengers, watching from the various upper decks. Apparently there was a clause in our contracts, at that time, which permitted the burial at sea of any crew member who died while at sea, unless of course, they had specifically adjusted their contract to the contrary. As a direct result of this one funeral, there were nearly a thousand crew members amending their contracts as soon as we docked in Southampton!

The procedure was relatively straight forward, when the corpse of any crew members was found, if the ship was more than twenty-four hours from docking, the ship's doctor was required to effect a post-mortem on the body to ensure that death was not due to foul play; if the latter is suspected, the area where the corpse was found was immediately sealed off until the ship docked and the police could investigate. If the circumstances were not suspicious, a death certificate was issued and the body was handed over to the bosun, who wrapped it in a canvass sheet. Some scraps of heavy metal were inserted to surround the corpse and to act as weights and ensure that the body was truly "committed to the deep", in other words, the body does not float on the surface but sinks to the seabed.

The whole thing was then sewn up and sealed, with the last stitch attaching the canvass to the forehead. This was a tradition dating back many hundreds of years and because of this fairly gruesome operation, it was a further long held tradition, to break out the rum, not only for the bosun , but also for the rest of the crew!

Finally, just prior to the commitment service, the body was placed upon a wooden board and covered with the Union Jack Flag. The pall bearers then carried the bier to the aft deck, where the Captain or Staff Captain conducted the burial service, and when the words, "…and we commit his body to the deep," the pall bearers lifted one end of the board and allowed the body to slip out from under the flag and into the sea. Naturally, such burials cannot take place in enclosed waters such as the Mediterranean Sea.

As you might expect, this death and the subsequent burial at sea, had a profound effect upon the whole crew, but it probably impacted more upon us youngsters, as for many of us, it was our first close up experience of death and there was no such thing as bereavement counselling to give us support in those days (men were men, because many of the crew still remembered the last World War). Just how profound an effect it was to have on me, did not become apparent until a couple of months later, when I was taken ill with a serious bout of suspected food poisoning.

We were less than twenty-four hours out of New York when I became ill. I was immediately rushed to the ship's infirmary, where at first they thought I had a suspected appendicitis. Luckily, this was soon dispelled and for the rest of our journey to New York, I was in and out of consciousness. I do, however, remember recovering semi-conscious as I was being wheeled down the gang plank on a stretcher. Upon seeing the sea below me, I was heard to scream, "No, I am not dead!"

Apparently, in my semi-conscious state, I thought the doctor had pronounced me dead and I was being buried at sea! A flashback to the burial at sea of the chef's secretary, I spent the next three days in hospital in New York and as a result of my extended stay, I missed the return sailing of the Queen Mary and consequently, I had to stay in that city until my ship returned two weeks later. This created problems of its own, as I neither had permission to stay in America and I therefore had to report to the police station every day. More importantly, to me anyway, I did not have any clothes other than the pyjamas I was wearing, when I was taken to hospital, nor did I have any money to pay for board and lodgings. Thank goodness the Company had signed "an acceptance of responsibility waiver" so I did not have to pay their hefty bill! Luckily a kind hospital visitor put me in touch with Jack Dempsey when I was released; yes that Jack Dempsey, the famous boxer, who had a Restaurant on 42nd Street, and he provided me with board and lodgings until my ship returned in exchange for my working in his restaurant. If he had not employed me, there would have been no alternative but for the police to have arrested me as an illegal immigrant and detained in prison until the ship returned, when I would have been deported.

This would also have meant that I could not return to the States as I would technically have had a criminal record, which in turn would have ended my career at sea.

Surprise, surprise, my first reaction was of sheer joy... two weeks in New York, just how good can life get, even if you do not have any money to fully explore the city, like me, you can always enjoy your own walking tours. So for the first three or four days of my stay, I was getting up in the morning and setting out on my voyage of discovery, complete with my tourists map, the Statue of Liberty (it is free), the Empire State Building (it was free), the cathedrals, the museums, Central Park etc. (all free). But after that, the novelty began to wear off and I found myself sleeping in longer and longer, so by the end of the first week I was becoming increasingly bored. I began to sleep until noon, then getting up and I made my way to the police station to make my daily report, which involved hanging around for at least two hours while some idiot tried to find my paperwork (you would think that as I had to report each day, my paper was near the top of someone's pile or perhaps that was the problem, no one knew whose pile my file was on!).

Those became the loneliest two weeks of my life as all I could really do was to work with the world's most boring and uncommunicative people, most of whom appeared to be Mexican or Puerto Rican and therefore spoke very little English – sorry American!

To make matters worse, the menu was so basic and boring and could be cooked by any "hash slinger" and in no way comparable to the gastronomic delights found on board, namely grilled steaks, burgers, salads and chips.

Eventually, the two weeks finally passed and I found myself once again standing on a quayside, waiting on the arrival of my ship. I have never been so happy to hear English voices again.

CHAPTER ELEVEN

One home trip in Southampton, the usual group of us went to a dance in the civic centre, mainly because it had a live group (well that is what it was advertised as!). We were very surprised to meet up with Keith, the fish cook from the ship, who was in his early twenties. He hailed from Somerset or Zummersett, as he pronounced it, and guess what we called him? Who told you? Well yes, OK, it was fairly obvious and some of us did lack imagination... oh, I did not tell you ,did I? Scrumpy, was his nickname, you know the rough cider from Somerset was called Scrumpy and he was a little on the rough side and came from Somerset, plus his favourite drink was cider! Keith was about 5 feet 10 inches tall and definitively a little overweight – unusual for a chef to be overweight – and he had a very dark complexion, and despite being a little rough, he was a nice guy really.

I think what surprised us, was the fact that he had a very attractive girlfriend, whom he introduced to us as Leila. What was even more surprising was something she let slip – she was not even drunk at the time. Scrumpy was going to smuggle her on board and help her stowaway to the States! When we had finished laughing, we suddenly realised that this was not a wind up and in actual fact, they (or Leila anyway) were deadly serious.

Leila was a surprisingly good looking young lady, given her choice of men (she could easily have done found a much more handsome fellow), she was slightly taller than Scrumpy and nowhere near as rotund as him; in fact, she was quite slim. She had jet black hair which flowed down her back to her waste, but her most striking feature was her pale blue feline eyes, which were magnificent. When she spoke, she almost purred as she was quietly spoken, which seemed even more appropriate, given her eyes. "So tell us how you are going to smuggle her on board," we mocked.

"Well, to start with, we have been waiting for the summer, so once on board she can hide in one of the lifeboats," said Scrumpy (I am sorry but it is very difficult to do the Somerset accent, especially when writing!).

"Yes, but how will you actually get her on board?" we asked, suddenly realising that they were serious. "You know how tight security is on sailing days, everyone is stopped and has to show their Seaman's Book to get on board."

"Ah yes, that is true, but on docking days they are more concerned with people coming off the ship and what they are carrying, rather than worrying about people going onto the ship," Scrumpy responded.

By now he had got our full attention, partly because we still could not believe what we hearing and partly because Scrumpy seemed to be the last person on God's earth you would suspect of being the mastermind behind such a major *crime*.

"Go on," we prompted.

"Leila wants to go to America to live, but unlike Australia, there is no such thing as assisted passage. Also, she would never get a green card, as she has no qualifications and no specific skills to offer. The cheapest fare we can find is over two hundred pounds – that's three months' pay! That is assuming she did not spend anything on rent or living; you know, bus fares, food... silly things like that ! So, the only answer is to smuggle her on board and hide her. It should be easy to feed her and as it is summer she will not get too cold in the lifeboat.

"But, it takes five days to sail to New York, what about a shower or going to the loo?" Angus asked, he always was the pragmatist.

"Never mind that, just exactly how are you going to get her on the ship in the first place?" I asked.

"I have made arrangements to get my hands on a stewardess's uniform from the laundry and I thought we would wait until all the crew began to leave the ship, then Leila and I would run back to the ship pretending we were late for our shift. Hopefully, we can sneak past the security guys as they busy themselves with the crew going ashore. I have tried this a couple of times already, and it works, if you time it right," explained Scrumpy.

"The big problem is how do I get my belongings on board? We really cannot think of a way," said Leila, hoping we might come up with a solution.

"If you put your stuff in smallish bags, then left them somewhere we could pick them up, we could bring them on board for you without raising suspicion. But you will need a suitcase when you get off in New York," suggested Angus.

I could not believe my ears; we were willingly colluding, nay, assisting a person to become a stowaway. If we got caught, we would be sacked, prosecuted, jailed, for what we were planning. Worse still, we actually were beginning to believe the whole thing was possible.

"Everyone ready for another round of bevies?" asked Kevin.

"Never mind another drink, should we be talking about this in public? You never know who is listening. Let's go somewhere less public," interjected Angus.

"We could go back to mine?" said Leila. "It's a bit small, but at least it is private. We can get a take away and some drinks on the way, if you like?"

So off we went to Leila's place, stopping off for some Chinese and lagers on the way.

Leila's claim that her place was a "bit small" was a indeed a gross understatement; it was one of the smallest bed-sits I have ever seen. It had an integral kitchen; well, two boiling rings with the smallest oven ever, and underneath and a toaster. We actually had to take it in turns to breath as it was so small! The easiest thing, was to push what little furniture there was to one side to create enough space, so we could at least sit on the floor. Further bad news, there was only one set of knives and forks and two plates.

Luckily, the food was no longer red hot and we could eat it with our fingers, and we drank the lagers straight from the can. We did not buy a party seven (sorry, this was a tin containing seven pints of beer/lager, into which one inserted a small gas cylinder and tap, which allowed you to pull off fresh pints!).

After our refreshments, the "plotters" continued to develop their infallible strategy to smuggle Leila on board and across the Atlantic, so that she could start her new life in the "New World" as she called it. By the end of the night, we had found a way to get her on board undetected; developed a plan to get her belongings on board; she would hide away in a lifeboat; food and drink would be smuggled up to her; all that remained was to solve the problem of how would June go to the toilet without being caught and how to get her off the ship?

Next day we all met up again, but sober this time, and we agreed that it was practically impossible for Leila to "hop in and out" of the lifeboat, every time she wanted a pee, without being seen by someone. Let's be honest, there was no way she could hold on for five days!

"I have been thinking," said Scrumpy. "My cabin is in the next block to the stewardess's and Colin (the guy who shares my cabin) is going on leave next trip. So, supposing Leila shared my cabin and we passed her off as an actual new stewardess, after all, we will have a uniform, so she could even go and help them with their work, so they won't moan.

That way my Glory Hole Steward will not catch her in my cabin or even have a reason to suspect anything. At meal times she could even come up to the kitchen and collect her food with the rest of the girls... who's going to know?"

"Would it not be better if we found out where there was an empty birth among the stewardesses and then on sailing day, one of us take Leila down to that cabin with the spare bunk and introduce her as a new hand ?" said Scrumpy. "That way, there would be less risk."

"Brilliant," enthused Leila. "But do you think I could pass myself off as a stewardess, though?"

"All you have to do is make beds and clean rooms; what is so hard about that?" asked Scrumpy. "If you are not sure, ask your roommate how they do things on this ship? She will only be too glad to show you the ropes, particularly if we tell everyone it is your first trip to sea and that you previously worked in a small hotel. Also, if you are ill during the trip, you would not have to panic, as you could stay in your *pit* unchallenged."

"But how do I get off the ship as I do not have a Seaman's Book?" asked Leila.

"The only thing I can think of is to bribe one of the porters to collect her case and escort Leila off the ship. You do have a passport don't you? That way you could simply go through immigration, telling them you were here on holiday. No, better still, you were in the States attending the wedding of your pen pal. Anyone have a contact name and address we can nominate as her sponsor while in the States and as her place of residence whilst in the country?" asked Angus. "Obviously, you would need some decent gear to mix in with the other *bloods* for when you went ashore, you know how the women all like to dress up when they leave the ship. Once clear of Immigration and Customs, one of us will meet you in the bar opposite the docks and help you find somewhere to stay."

"I know a family who have a daughter of the right age, who live in New Jersey." said Kevin. "We could use their name and address, if necessary."

"What happens if I get caught?" Leila asked nervously.

"They will just send you back to England. For Christ sake, do not tell them that any of us helped you; if they ever discover any of us helped you, we would be blacklisted for life and would never be able to enter the States again, either for work or for holidays," added Angus.

"Good point. If you did get caught, how about telling them that you have been planning this for months, meeting various stewardesses in pubs in Southampton where you knew they went, and you were able to chat to them about life at sea. That way you were able to obtain information about the ship's procedures. They even told who had a spare bunk in their cabin. Then just before you were ready to proceed, one of the girls was so drunk that she left her bag behind, which contained her uniform," suggested Scrumpy.

So everything was arranged, Scrumpy and Leila decided to go for it in ten days' time when we next docked in Southampton. In the meantime, we would try and find out where there might be a vacant bunk amongst the stewardesses. The best person to ask was Aunt Peggy, known to be the oldest woman working on the ship, who got her nickname because she was a spinster who mothered everyone. She was a lovely lady, but she was extremely naïve, some people even described her as been "soft", nevertheless, she always meant well.

One lunchtime Scrumpy saw the opportunity to chat to Aunt Peggy and he was eventually able to work the conversation around to the crews accommodation.

"You girls are housed up near the officers, aren't you? Do you have large multi-person cabins or do you have a room to yourselves?"

"Yes, we are in the same corridor as the catering senior ratings. We all share a cabin with one other girl, everyone, that is, except me. I haven't had a roommate for ages. I do not know why," she replied.

"I am sorry to hear that," lied Scrumpy, when in reality he was inwardly shouting BINGO to himself. That was the last piece to the jigsaw. Leila could be taken down to Aunt Peggy's. She would be ideal; she would love the company, and she would not ask too many questions and she would love to show her the ropes. Lady luck was certainly shining down on them; everything seemed to be falling into place and he suddenly felt enormous confidence in the whole plan. Surely, nothing could go wrong?

Scrumpy admitted that that was the longest trip he had ever made, but it was just five days as usual. Before docking in New York, we set about finding out how to rent accommodation for Leila; this was quite easy, as many of the crew had places they rented in the city. As soon as we docked, the three of us visited the three rental agencies people had told us about. Luckily, we had been pre-warned that we would need to pay three months up front; ideally, we would have to give references in the UK and we would have to sign a one-year contract; accordingly, the property was to be put in Scrumpy's name, as it might be too risky to put it in Leila's name.

At the end of the day, we could not believe how easy it actually was for us, not only to find a furnished apartment, in a reasonable neighbourhood, at a reasonable rental and with few questions being asked. Yes, we did indeed find a place which fulfilled all our requirements; we viewed the place, completed the paperwork, conducted a stock take on its contents... all of which we completed in one day! It took Scrumpy two weeks to do exactly the same thing in England. That night we went out to celebrate, we even stayed the night in his new place, forgetting we did not have any shopping in, not even the ingredients for a cuppa!

When we docked in Southampton, Scrumpy was one of the first people off the ship, which was not difficult as we docked at lunchtime and everyone else was engaged either in preparing/serving lunch or in eating it. You can imagine his relief at seeing Leila waiting at the agreed place, complete with all her personal belongings, which they duly sorted out and placed the surplus in the left luggage locker next to the docks, as agreed.

They then went to the café, to wait for the first crew members to start disembarking, so they could put part two of their plan into operation.

It was not long before the crew members – and the stewardesses in particular – began to disembark. This was their signal to get ready to move and they began to make their way to the dock gates. As they approached the gates, Scrumpy could feel himself sweating or was it perspiring? But today was their day, just as they arrived at the gate, one of the departing crewmen was discovered to have something wrong with his paperwork and they were able to walk straight through without a glance: stage two successfully completed. As soon as it was safe to start running without attracting too much attention, they made a dash for the crew's gangplank.

"You know what to do now?" asked Scrumpy.

"Of course I do!" she hissed in a most impatient manner. "Sorry, I am scared stiff."

"No problem. Look there is a queue, let's go!" he replied.

With that, they run up the gangplank and once again their luck held as they were waved straight through.

"Keep going! Just follow me," Scrumpy whispered, as he led her away from the gangplank and towards the staircase that led to the stewardess's cabins: stage three successfully completed.

At the foot of the stairs, they stopped to regain their breath; both their hearts were beating like tom toms, partly with excitement and partly through sheer terror, it was all going too well! Once they had resumed their composure, they went over the plans for the final phase of their plan, then, taking a deep breath, they made their way towards Aunt Peggy's cabin.

"Aunt Peggy, are you there?" shouted Scrumpy. "I found your new roommate wandering around the ship and so I have brought her down. Show her the ropes will you? She seems very green to me."

With that, the cabin door opened, and a beaming Aunt Peggy appeared, dressed in the oldest quilted dressing gown you have ever seen – even the flowers had faded!

"Hello, darling," she said. "Come on in. My name is Peggy; everybody calls me Aunt Peggy. What's your name? Do you fancy a cuppa? Have you had breakfast? Have you been to sea before?" and so she went on, firing question after question, but without waiting for an answer, so great was her excitement – a cabin mate at last.

Eventually she stopped for breath and Leila was able to get in.

"My name is Leila, this is the first time I have ever been to sea. I have had breakfast but would love a cuppa." Then turning to Scrumpy she said, "Thank you so much for your help. By the way, what is your name?"

"My name is Keith, but everyone calls me Scrumpy. I'll see you around, have fun," he said, trying to be totally nonchalant and cool. With that he made his exit and once outside he punched the air: stage four completed successfully! He could not wait to get up to the kitchen to tell us how well the day had gone.

As soon as he was out the door, Leila said, "What a nice guy. Is he married? Do you know if he has a girlfriend?" God she had only been with Peggy for thirty minutes and she was already sounding like Peggy!

"His name is Scrumpy because he comes from Somerset. I have never heard him talking about a wife or girlfriend. Why, do you fancy him?"

"I would not mind," replied Leila.

Poor Leila, if only Scrumpy had realised what he was letting Leila in for... not that there was anything he could have done about it. However, it soon became apparent to Leila though, as to why Peggy had never had a cabin mate, or as to why she had never got married. Peggy never stopped, from the moment she got up until the time she went to bed! It did not stop there as she wanted to take Leila into town for a night out, but luckily, Leila put her off without offending her or arousing her suspicions, by pretending to be very tired and needing to sort herself out for work next day, you know, women's things like showering, washing her hair, doing her nails etc.

For the rest of the trip, she fussed around Leila like a sheepdog does around a flock of errant sheep. She woke her up in the mornings with a cuppa; she took her to work; she showed her the ropes (accepting Leila's lack of knowledge and skills as being purely down to the fact that she had only worked in inferior hotels), and she arranged her meals and sorted her laundry (she even managed to get her extra uniforms after Leila claimed to have left her spares at home). So attentive was Peggy that we found it extremely difficult to get the rest of Leila's belongings, which we had collected from the left luggage locker, back to her without Peggy seeing us. The suitcase was particularly difficult and in the end, we had to return it through that section's glory hole steward.

We told him some cock and bull story about her leaving it behind in her taxi and not being able to find out who it belonged to.

Scrumpy and Leila did manage to snatch the odd moment together during the trip, but both longed desperately for the trip to end. However, the day before docking there was a sudden panic; we had overlooked a couple of major things. How would Leila be able to gather all her belongings together without Peggy seeing her and becoming suspicious?

How would she get her suitcase out of the cabin and up to a porter, again, without attracting attention? Then on docking day, how could she get all dressed up and make her way into the passenger accommodation? Worse still, how would we account for Leila's absence on the return trip? Time for another planning meeting; we just could not fall at the last fence.

The only thing we could think of was for Leila to go sick, twenty-four hours before docking, which would then give her both the time and the opportunity to pack while Peggy was at work. All she had to do was to remember to keep her "posh" clothes out and to keep her locker locked, so Peggy could not see into her wardrobe. Behind the cover of illness, plus her knowledge of Peggy's routine, Leila could also use this time to find an unused cabin in which she could hide her suitcase. It would then be ready for the porter to collect too.

Then, on docking day, after Peggy had gone to work, Leila could leave a note for her saying she was going to see a doctor ashore. She could then get herself dressed and once we had docked, make her way to the vacant cabin, from where she could summon a porter to carry her luggage ashore. Naturally, she needed to have her passport and the wedding details to hand, ready for the American immigration.

Finally, Scrumpy would have to see Peggy before we set sail on our return trip, and explain that Leila had appendicitis and was having an operation, and therefore, she would not be making the return trip. We would also have to remember to tell her that Leila had been returned home on another ship because of an infection, caught during her stay in hospital. *Result!* All buttoned up, all we now had to do was to put the plan into operation.

Destiny appeared to be on our side, as one evening, Scrumpy found the opportunity to talk to the ship's nurse, claiming to have a pain in his stomach and asking if it could be appendicitis. The nurse pressed around his stomach and explained the symptoms for appendicitis; naturally, they were nothing like Scrumpy's pain, and so they concluded he had severe bouts of indigestion. He even got some tablets off the nurse for future use. This information was to be put to good use, but not in the way the nurse had envisaged; he was actually able to give Peggy accurate symptoms for Leila's phantom bout of appendicitis.

D-day came for Leila, the day before we were due to dock, she woke up and told Peggy she felt really rough and, according to plan, Peggy told her to stay in bed. Once it was safe, Leila carefully packed her suitcase and returned it to her wardrobe; for some reason she resisted the urge to take it to the empty passenger's cabin she had found earlier in the trip. Her intuition was rewarded when ten minutes later Peggy popped back to check on how she was feeling. Bless her, she even brought a cup of tea for Leila. Having satisfied herself everything was alright, Peggy went back to work, although she sought out the steward on the way and asked him not to disturb Leila. What an extra bonus!

This totally left the way clear for Leila to sneak her luggage up to the passenger accommodation and hide it without being seen; however, she was seen by a crew member on her way back down to her cabin, but luckily she was in her uniform and all that happened was the other person simply said "hello" as she passed.

As expected, the next day was as chaotic as any other docking day. Peggy rushed off to see her passengers before they left the ship; well, some of them had not tipped her yet!

All the rest of the crew were rushing around trying to finish their work as quickly as possible, so that they could maximise their shore leave. We of course had other reasons; one of us had to be on deck when Leila tried to get ashore in case something went wrong (although I am still not sure what we were supposed to do if it had gone wrong).

Perhaps we were all supposed to do a runner?

Anyway, Leila dressed herself in all her finery: clothes, make up, posh hairstyle and a lovely little carry case, and then she carefully opened the cabin door enough to see the corridor. As soon as it was clear, she slipped out and carefully made her way to the passenger cabin which contained her suitcase. All went well and she made it safely, without being found out. She opened the cabin door and almost fell in, so great was her relief; well, once she had visited the loo she felt a lot better! She watched in utter terror from the porthole, waiting for passengers to start disembarking, hoping against hope, that no one decided to check that this particular cabin was indeed ready for its new occupants on the return sailing.

Finally, the trickle turned to a steady stream; it was time to go. She picked up the telephone, her hand was shaking so much that it seemed to rattle against her jaw! She dialled the number to summon the porter, her voice quivered nervously; would they suspect something? She felt blind panic as a voice from the other end of the phone asked for her cabin number, but her mind was blank... what was the f*****g number? "Just a minute," she heard herself say, "there is someone at the door."

With that she rushed to the door, opened it, read the number and then rushed back to the phone.

"Sorry about that. Now, where were we? My cabin number is 231 on C deck. How long will you be? Ten minutes will be fine."

But her nerves were getting the better of her, and after five minutes, she decided to move her case into the corridor and take a chance of waiting outside, rather than risk being caught in the supposedly empty cabin. After what seemed an absolute age, a porter eventually arrived.

"My friend has gone on," she lied.

"OK, ma'am," replied the porter, picking up her suitcase and placing it on his trolley.

"Right, let's go. Is this your first trip to the States?" he asked.

"Yes," Leila replied.

"Immigration is a bit of a pain" – nothing has changed there then! – "But it should not to take too long."

Off they went, the porter leading the way. Leila was petrified by this stage in case one of the stewardesses recognised her as they made their way to the lounge area being used by immigration. When they arrived, there was a small queue and so she did not have to wait too long. The porter kept speaking to her; well, if he was nice, the bigger the tip he hoped to get, but she was almost oblivious to everything he said. Suddenly, she was aware that the immigration man in front of her was calling her forward.

"Sorry," she said, "I was miles away."

"What is the purpose of your visit?" he asked.

"I am attending my pen pal's wedding," she replied.

"Is this your first visit?" he went on.

"Yes, I have been saving for nearly two years for this trip," she said, trying extremely hard to appear calm.

"Have you ever been arrested? Do you have a criminal record? Do you take drugs?" he asked.

"No. I have never been arrested and so do not have a criminal record. I have never taken drugs either," she answered.

"How long are you staying and do you have an address for while you are here?" he asked.

"Here is my address. I am staying with my friend at her home and I am staying for two weeks," Leila replied.

"OK," he said as he stamped and returned her passport. "Have a nice stay."

"Where do we go now?" Leila asked her porter.

"We leave the ship and then go through Customs," he replied.

The next thing she knew was, they were walking down the gangplank having been bid a fond farewell from an officer, who acted as if he recognised her; if only he knew or rather, remembered, he was playing cards and bingo with her only two nights ago in the Officer's Mess. Customs was a mere formality and she virtually walked through, without any trouble. She was home and dry, or so she thought, as she handed over a sizable tip to her loyal but grateful porter. The next thing she knew, her luggage was being piled into the boot of a bus by the driver and she was being ushered towards the front of the bus by her porter.

"What's going on? Where is this bus taking us to?" she almost screamed.

"It takes everyone to the Cunard's depot downtown," he replied, pushing her onto the bus.

Leila did not wish to cause a rumpus at this stage and so she climbed onto the bus and took a seat; after all, I can always get a taxi back to Pete's (the bar we all agreed to meet in), it will just take a bit longer. What she did not realise was that Scrumpy was watching proceedings from the crew deck of the ship and when he saw her disappear onto the bus, he totally flipped out. He rushed down to the kitchen to let us know what was happening and then went to his cabin, grabbed his seaman's card and wallet and headed for the staff gangplank, but of course he had not been cleared by American immigration to go ashore this trip and so he was refused permission to go ashore. He frantically dashed up to the crew deck to get his shore leave docket, and guess what? There was a queue of some twenty crew members!

By the time it came to his turn, the bus had long since gone. In desperation, he rushed round to where he had last seen the bus, where he asked one of the porters still hanging around where the bus had gone. Upon being told it had taken everyone to the downtown office, he jumped into the nearest taxi; it was almost a "follow that bus moment", and set off in pursuit of his beloved Leila. Naturally, by the time he arrived at the Cunard office, Leila had grabbed a cab of her own and was heading back to the designated meeting place. Talk about your "Keystone Cops" (sorry young people, they were stars of the silent movies, who hared about the place, causing absolute mayhem everywhere they went).

There was nothing left to do, but to return to Pete's and wait, and hope that eventually Leila would find her way back there (I do not know what Scrumpy was thinking, his beloved was one of the most intelligent women I had met in a long while and it was a piece of cake for her to find her way back to the agreed meeting place), particularly as she had a reasonable amount of dollars in her possession.

By the time she got back to Pete's, both Angus and I were in the bar, waiting for them to return. Fortunately, it was too early in the day for the majority of the crew to also be there and better still, none of the stewardesses were there. Imagine our relief when we saw Leila getting out of her cab, fully expecting Scrumpy to appear from the other side, of course. But there was no sign of him, and so we both dashed out to find out what had happened, which of course Leila knew very little about. So we all went into the bar to await Scrumpy, who duly obliged by appearing some ten minutes later.

God, how we celebrated, not just the fact that we had all found each other, but also the fact that we had successfully managed to smuggle Leila on board, helped her to stowaway for five days, aided her illegal access into

America, and all undetected by either the shipping company or the American immigration – we were geniuses!

Once we had regained our sanity, we suddenly realised the risks we were running by remaining so close to the ship in broad daylight, anyone could recognise Leila and bring us all down. We quickly caught a cab and set off for Leila's new apartment, and we spent the rest of the day shopping for food and all the other essentials needed... you know, the simple things like toilet paper etc. That night we had the biggest party ever; after all, we were all chefs! At the end of the evening, Angus and I returned to the ship, basking in the fact that we were the first people to smuggle a stowaway on board the Queen undetected.

By the time Scrumpy returned to the ship next day, he had organised a job for Leila in a hotel as a chambermaid, which paid enough money for her to live on (in those days, it was very difficult to recruit hotel staff and consequently, the hotels were extremely lax about checking the legality of their employees... gosh, that sounds familiar!).

We saw Scrumpy from time to time and he kept us informed about how well his partner was doing and how well their relationship was progressing. I remember this liaison continued until I left the ship and I like to think that they lived happily ever after. I know, yuk, I'm an old romantic!

CHAPTER TWELVE

It had not been a good couple of weeks for me, despite having been on leave for most of that time, mainly because the weather had been crap, but I suppose one should expect bad weather at the end of September. All my mates had either gone off to University or moved away for work during my absence. The summer season had finished in the town and so there were no foreign students or holiday makers, so Eastbourne seemed to be dead and extremely boring, and to be honest, I was glad when eventually my leave was finally over. But my woes did not end there as my bike broke down on the way back to Southampton and it took me absolutely ages to fix it, mainly due to the fact that I did not know what I was doing, but officially because I did not have the right tools to fix the problem. As a result, I was over two hours' late reporting back on duty.

As a direct consequence of my tardiness, I was invited to see the head chef, an honour indeed, I don't think!

"What is your excuse this time, son? Not that I am really interested, it's just that I like to stretch your imagination," he enquired sarcastically.

"I am so sorry, chef, but my bike broke down on the way back to Southampton and I had to thumb a lift into the nearest garage to get some help and by the time I got it finished I was extremely late..."

"Not bad," he interrupted. "But you should have left earlier; after all, you have just had ten days' leave, you idle little bugger. Why didn't you leave last night to give yourself a margin and make certain you were back in time?"

"But, chef, I would still have broken down and would not have been able to get any help as all the garages would have been shut." Good, quick thinking I thought to myself.

"Not my problem," he interrupted. "This is not the first time we have had to have words is it, and you are still a pain in the arse! Well, this is your last chance, any more problems and you can sling your hook. But you are not getting away with it this time; this trip you will work on the Roast Corner with Yogi and perhaps we can sweat some sense into you. Now get out! I've got better things to do with my time," he rasped.

I left with a great sense of relieve as the chef had obviously forgotten that this was exactly what he said last time he banished me to the Roast Corner and I was extremely fortunate not to have been thrown off the ship there and then as he had done to previous deviants appearing before him.

As you can imagine, my trip to New York was very hard, because it was just my luck that the ship had a full complement of passengers and the Roast Corner was naturally the busiest section of the kitchen anyway. Then of course there was the heat and the essential salt tablets that accompanied this heat. However, the gods had not deserted me completely, because from the moment we left Cherbourg, we met very rough seas, restricting many passengers to their cabins with seasickness and dehydration, all of which helped to reduce their appetite and the pressure upon us.

Despite the weather, we arrived on time at the mouth of the Hudson on October 2nd, and I thought my luck had changed further when I won $10 in the sweepstake for picking the correct arrival time at the Nab Bell Tower (the permanent floating shipping lane marker at the mouth of the Hudson,) but this was a temporary lapse as I was soon to discover.

The river pilot and tugs joined us as usual and guided us down river to our usual pier berth to assist with the docking of this huge ship. Simultaneously, as the lunch service had finished, one of our chores was to strain all the fritures (pans used for deepfat frying) used during the lunch service to cook deep fried fish and chips. This had to be done while the fat was still hot (325 degrees F minimum or 190 C in new money) and involved one person holding a conical strainer lined with muslin while a second person carefully pours out the hot fat from the friture. On this occasion, I was pouring and Angus was squatting down holding the strainer.

What we did not know was the fact that the long shore men who manned the tugs were called out on an immediate strike, which resulted in them cutting through the hawsers with axes and casting the Queen Mary adrift in the Hudson, as the ship's engines had been cut once the tugs took control. As if this was not bad enough, apparently we were left at an angle of some 30 degrees and we were drifting dangerously down river, risking either running aground or capsizing. Consequently, Captain Watts had no option than to continue the berthing without the tugs and so he restarted his engines and attempted to dock the 87,000 tonnes of floating metal.

Although this manoeuvre was mainly successful, he did collide with the pier with a violent bump, which naturally threw me off balance. I was later told that I tried to steady the friture in an attempt to prevent the hot fat from spilling over Angus's head, but in doing so, caused the fat to spill over both my hands, "welding" them to the pan handles.

As you can imagine, I remember none of this as I passed out.

When they removed the pan from my hands, they also removed several layers of skin and I was rushed to the ship's infirmary. Unfortunately, the doctor was at the traditional Docking Day Party and was busy treating several passengers who had been injured by the collision, although these were mainly minor cuts and bruises coupled with minor shock.

As a consequence, the Charge Hand Nurse plunged both my hands into surgical spirits, which apparently was the standard treatment for burns at that time. This resulted in my hands swelling up like balloons because of the blistering and so the nurse lanced these blisters.

Eventually the doctor was able to return to the infirmary, where he examined my hands and then immediately summoned an ambulance. As the gurney carried me down the gangway, apparently I regained semi-consciousness, being in the unconscious position (namely on my side) all I can remember is seeing the sea beneath me and screaming, "I am not dead!" a reference to witnessing the burial at sea of the chef's valet.

My two medics had to struggle to prevent me from tipping the gurney over and ending up in the sea; thankfully I was strapped onto the gurney and they managed to get me to the shore before I tipped into the sea. I later discovered that my two medics were called John and Wayne... only I could get the services of a world famous film star to rush me to hospital. I suppose I should be grateful that they came by ambulance and not by stagecoach!

I spent the whole of the following week alone in a strange hospital in New York, drifting in and out of consciousness and drugged up to the eyeballs. Both my hands were covered in bandages and in suspended slings to prevent further damage, which made it impossible for me to do anything for myself and that included eating, drinking and going to the toilet.

At the end of the week, just when I was feeling a bit better, I had a visitor from the National Union of Seamen, who came to tell me that I was being transferred to the Queen Elizabeth and being repatriated to the UK. I expect the company was running out of money keeping me in hospital like this! He went on to tell me that he would be overseeing my recuperation and compensation claim, all of which we could discuss on the trip home as he was a steward on the ship.

So began the long journey to my rehabilitation. I was transported to the docks by ambulance (no John Wayne this time) with both hands bandaged up past the wrists. It was then that I noticed my dress or rather the absence of dress (no I am not a transvestite) when I was admitted to hospital. Apparently, I was only wearing my chef's uniform and they had to cut my jacket off in order to treat me, which naturally totalled it. As I had had no visitors in the meanwhile, I had no access to replacement clothes (the hospital even kept the gown they gave me). Thankfully, I still had my chef's trousers and a blanket wrapped around me to protect my modesty, as they pushed me up the gangplank on a gurney.

At the top of the gangplank, we were greeted by the Master of Arms who demanded to see my National Union of Seaman's ID Card (these replaced Passports for Seamen).

"Sorry, I was rushed off to hospital as an emergency and did not have time to go to my cabin to gather my belongings, that's why I am dressed this way."

"So how am I supposed to verify who you are?" he asked.

"Look it was one of you crew who was supposed to organise my trip back to England. He is an NUS Official and works as a steward. He came to hospital yesterday and told me everything was arranged," I replied.

"Do you know that there are some 1,200 crew members on this ship and over 100 are stewards! So what was his name?" he asked.

"I am sorry, he did not tell me his name, so I haven't a clue," I lamented.

While all this was going on, quite an audience had gathered, comprising of both passengers waiting to get on the ship and those already on board, and it is fair to say that those on the gangplank were becoming restless, to put it mildly, having spent a fortune on their fare. Then to rub salt into the wound (not literally of course), the two medics joined in

"Say, Mac, we can't hang around here all day while you decide what you are going to do with this guy; we do have other work waiting you know. We ain't taking him back, that's for sure, so you either allow him on board or we just tip him off our gurney right here and now," said the driver.

Just then a "two ringer" (an officer) appeared and angrily demanded to know what the hold up was.

"This man claims to be a crewman from the Mary, whom we are supposed to take back to England. But he has no ID, no ticket or authorisation, and does not even know the name of the person who is organising the whole thing. I have been told nothing about this. He could be a bum looking for a cheap trip home for all I know," said the Master.

"Use your common sense, man, and take him somewhere in private and sort it out, but for goodness sake allow these *bloods* to board the ship. Just get him out the way right now," he hissed between clenched teeth.

"But I only have my chef's trousers on under this blanket. I do not even have any shoes," I cried in desperation.

"Bloody hell! Just push him into that office over there, right now," demanded the officer. Then get someone to organise some clothes and shoes for him, Master, and get those *bloods* on board." Then, turning to the crowd he said, "Ladies and gentlemen, my apologies for the delay, we will recommence your boarding immediately."

By the time he had finished speaking, I had been wheeled into the nominated office, stripped of my blanket and dumped off the gurney by the two medics, who then disappeared out the door, with their gurney and blanket of course. The Master also disappeared, leaving a rather large and menacing sailor by the door to ensure that I did not do a runner.

A couple of minutes later, the Staff Captain arrived and held out his hand to welcome me aboard, upon realising my predicament he diverted his hand to scratch his head – clever, but a bit obvious.

"Whoops! Sorry, old chap, sorry about the cock up, breakdown in communications don't you know. Do you know where we are putting you? Is it the infirmary, a passenger cabin or crew quarters?" he asked.

"I am sorry, sir, I do not have a clue about what is going on. Just like you, I have not been told anything about the arrangements," I said apologetically.

It was at that moment that the Master returned with a T-shirt and a pair of disposable slippers. "Here we go," he said. "Just pop these on."

"No chance," I said, waving my bandaged hands in front of his face.

"Give him a hand, Master, there's a good chap," smiled the Staff Captain, "then get the Doc on the phone for me."

"Yes, sir," replied the Master, placing the slippers in a convenient position for me to slip into.

"Excuse me, sir, can someone help me go to the toilet," I said.

"There is one next door," replied the Master.

"But I cannot undo my flies or..." I exclaimed.

"For crying out loud, either get him down to the infirmary or get one of their bods up here immediately!" screamed the Staff Captain.

Strange how the problems of my identity had suddenly disappeared and the new priority was who was going to take me to the toilet! What a welcome to the sister ship, the Queen Elizabeth, a total let down, they could not organise a piss up in a brewery! It just made me so thankful that I was not allocated to this ship when I first joined the Merchant Navy.

So off we went to the infirmary, down the backstairs of course, and once there the Master just seemed to disappear. I did not even see the puff of smoke, probably terrified by the prospect of having to take me to the toilet.

The Senior Orderly, Bert, introduced himself before taking me to the toilet and helping me into bed and getting me settled, ready for the arrival of the Doc. I was then presented with a three-course meal, with Bert doing the honours and feeding me. Shortly after finishing my lunch, the Doc finally arrived.

"OK, young man. Sorry what was your name? Mike. OK, Mike, now tell me what happened and how you ended up in this mess," he began.

I told him everything I could, which was not very much as I had not had the opportunity to speak to anyone on the Queen Mary.

"Right then. When was the last time they changed your dressing? Do you know what they dressed the wounds with and have they given you any medication?" he asked.

"My dressings were changed just before I left hospital when they put some form of cream onto the gauze before loosely placing it onto my hands. They then wrapped the whole thing up with the bandages. I really do not know how often the dressings were changed as I was barely conscious for a lot of the time. The last couple of days I have been given some kind of tablet four times a day. I believe they might have been some form of pain killers, apart from that, I do not really know much more, I am afraid," I lamented.

"Great, that helps. I do not think there is any point in removing the dressings just yet. I think it would be better leaving it for a couple of days. How bad is the pain? Can you describe it?" asked the Doc.

"They do not hurt at the moment, probably because I had a tablet just before leaving the hospital, but once they start to wear off, both hands can be really painful."

"I believe you left hospital less than a couple of hours ago, so there is no immediate urgency. Bert will you phone the hospital and find out what cream they were using and what painkillers they were administering together with the details of their strength... you know, the usual stuff. It would be helpful if they could also courier over their notes and details of treatment to date. Tell them to add the cost to their bill," he instructed. "In the meanwhile, I will see you later today and leave you in the capable hands of Bert."

The one good thing about being in hospital was one could listen to the radio. Remember this was the early sixties, and the Beatles first record (Love Me Do) had only just reached number one in the British Charts, and so television was not readily available to the masses. The only problem was you did not have control of the controls and were stuck with the channel the staff wanted to listen to, but this was still better than nothing and helped pass the time. Despite this, time passed very slowly and the only thing to look forward to was your next meal!

A bit later that afternoon, Bert returned to tell me that he had received my notes from the hospital and they now knew what painkillers were working. He also told me that my hands had been examined by one of America's leading burn specialists and he believed that the nerve ends in my hands had been badly damaged and this could mean that I would have no feelings in my hands. The good news was that the damage was mainly restricted to my palms and the skin did not appear to be irreversibly damaged, that being the case, I would not require skin grafts. The only potential problem was, I did not have any fingerprints, which would not please the American Immigration Department and could prevent me from going ashore, but this needed checking.

However, my recovery would be very slow... over many months, even years before all the damage would be fully repaired although my fingerprints should return sooner.

Later on in the early evening, I received my first visitor, not exciting though as it was only the guy from the NUS who came to see me in hospital.

"Hi there, how are you doing? Sorry I was not here when you arrived but I was on shore leave." Nice to know what your priorities are, I thought to myself. "So, where do we go from here?" he enquired.

"Well, you can begin by telling me your name," I started.

"Of course, sorry, my name is John. I have only just started this Union business and so it is all new to me. I was only elected as the ship's rep at the beginning of the month, but it is something I have always really wanted to get into. Sorry, I am waffling, what have the doctors told you about your injuries?"

"While I was in hospital, I was apparently seen by one of America's top specialists in burns, who believes that my nerve ends are damaged beyond repair, but the good news is that my skin could well recover without the need for any grafting. At the moment I do not have any fingerprints, although who the hell would know under all this bandaging, I do not know. His best prognosis is that recovery will be a long slow process and could take up to a year before things return to anywhere near normality," I reported.

"Ouch! That does not sound good," he said, "so I need to find out from the Union as to what your options are. I will send them a radiogram straight away and we should get a reply within the next couple of days. What is obvious is that you are not going to be able to use your hands for the foreseeable future; that should not be too much of a problem on the ship as we can arrange support but it will be a totally different matter when you are ashore," *talk about stating the obvious!*

"Things should be a bit clearer in the next couple of days when the ship's doctor changes my dressings, as he has not actually seen my hands as yet," I advised John.

"OK then, Mike, we have a plan. I will approach headquarters on your behalf and pop back in a couple of days with their advice. By then the Doc will have had the opportunity to examine your hands and he might know more then. Is there anything you need?" he asked.

"I do need some clothes, preferably some loose fitting trousers, T-shirts and a pair of slip on shoes as it would be really nice to get some fresh air as I cannot go anywhere dressed like this. Also, how long am I going to be stuck here in the infirmary as there is no one to talk to except Bert and he is not here half the time. Do you know if I am being transferred to a cabin of some sort?" I replied.

"Again this is something I need to ask, so be patient... oops , sorry about the pun. I'll be in touch," and with that he was off, without even saying goodbye!

The next couple of days were extremely long and boring, particularly as I still could not do anything for myself from shaving to bathing, eating or drinking... not even going to the toilet without help, and neither could I even read a book as there was no way of turning the pages. One improvement that had been made was the setting up of a cup with a lid and straw, which did allow me to access a cold drink. None of which was helped by the fact that no clothes had appeared, which prevented me from even going anywhere.

By the third day of boredom, I was beginning to climb the bulkheads – walls to you. I believe I had even started to talk to myself! When all of a sudden a strange apparition appeared before me, a figure covered from head to foot in a green garb, complete with a green mask. It was the Doc. He had come to change my dressings. If this was not bad enough, quick on his heels, came Bert, dressed exactly the same: two for one don't you know.

"We are going to change your dressings now," said the Doc and they immediately set about removing my bandages. This was the first time I had seen my hands since the accident and it was not a pretty sight. My fingers resembled little fat pinky/red, raw sausages – ugh! The palms of my hands were also red raw and reminded me of a couple of raw steaks. You can tell I am a chef as everything reminds me of food.

Despite taking the utmost care in the removal of my dressing, this proved to be quite a painful experience and I am afraid I did resort to letting out a couple of winces during the process. The final piece of dressing was held in place just above my wrists, with sticky tape and when he removed it, he tore volumes of hair from my arms, leaving a track similar to that left by a watch strap after sunbathing. Naturally, this provoked a further yelp through gritted teeth. Finally, it was finished, giving the Doc his first sight of my wounds.

"I must say, they are not as bad as I thought they would be and as there are actually no open wounds, we can dispense with all this garb," and promptly removed both their masks and hats. "That's much better. Yes, several layers of your skin has been stripped off; did you know that you have seven layers of skin and that the top layer is actually dead and is being replaced all of the time. The damage to the back of your hands is minimal, but still looks very painful," he concluded.

The redressing of my wounds followed the tried and tested method of applying cream to gauze, and holding it in place with the bandages; thankfully, the application was less painful than the removal.

"Do you fancy a cuppa? Sorry it cannot be anything stronger, but the painkillers do not allow alcohol. Bert will you do the honours. We will change them again in three to four days and I'll see you then," he said.

A short time later John appeared bearing gifts, several T-shirts, a pair of trousers and a pair of sabots (wooden shoes worn in professional kitchens).

"Sorry for the delay, but I had someone in housekeeping modify the trousers, putting elastic in the waist and some sticky tape (Velcro to us), which will stick to your bandages and allow you to pull your pants up and down using the back of your hands. If you go "commando", you should virtually be able to dress and undress yourself and even go to the loo by yourself, which will be less embarrassing.

I have also heard back from the Union and it appears that you have a couple of options. Namely, when we dock, go home for a week to await the arrival of the Mary. When you rejoin, you will be given a commis chef to act as your hands. You tell him what to do and he will do it. That way you will continue to receive your full pay, shore leave etc. The second option is for you to go home until your wounds are fully healed, in which case you will only receive the statutory sick pay. Naturally in either case, the Union will continue to represent you in seeking compensation both for any loss of wages and for damages for injuries caused, to be assessed once you are fully recovered. It goes without saying that you will always have a job with Cunard. I should also add that the NUS is a closed shop, which means you cannot take any form of action against the company except through the Union. So what do you think then?" asked John.

After a few minutes of contemplation, and, remembering my total boredom, caused by inactivity over the past week or so and what a disaster my recent leave had been, I decided to give the working option a try. Which I communicated to John.

"A couple of things... have you sorted out whether I stay here or move to some other accommodation? What will happen to my bike in Southampton as I will not be able to ride it for ages? Will you sort out a travel warrant for me to go home to Eastbourne and return to join the Mary?" I asked.

"It looks like you will have to stay here until we dock, but now you have some clothes, you are free to use the crew facilities. I will ask about the bike and travel warrant.

Anything else?"

"Not at present," I responded.

Well that is what happened. I stayed in the infirmary until docking, managed to get out on deck (was it cold though) and sat in the Pig drinking orange juice through a straw, not knowing anyone and speaking to a limited number of curious souls who wanted to know what had happened to me. John was as good as his word, organising for my bike to be shipped home for me and actually managed to arrange a travel warrant.

When I got home, I was dismayed to find out that no one had thought to tell my parents about my accident and they were horrified and shocked to see me arrive home in a taxi with two bandaged hands, dressed in a T-shirt, trousers wooden slip on shoes and an ill fitting heavy coat! But at least I had access to my own clothes, even if I could not put them on by myself. Needless to say, the week dragged by as I feared. But at least I had someone to talk to and my GP was more than happy to change my dressings; this time it did not seem so painful.

CHAPTER THIRTEEN

Five days had passed since my return home, although it still seemed strange to be sleeping in the "guest room" rather than in my own room which had been commandeered by my younger brother, after all, we lived in a council house on a council estate, not Buck House. Now it was time for me to say farewell to everyone and to be on my way, only this time by train and not on my bike as usual.

I had several issues to resolve as I still had very little use of my hands; the first of which was I could not carry a suitcase and so my mother had borrowed a haversack (a wartime sack with straps worn over the shoulders) from a neighbour. At least this way I could transport both the temporary clothes issued by the Union and my own spare clothes without having to worry about my hands.

The second potential problem was, how do I pay my bus fare, as I could not get my hand in and out of my pocket? Once again, Mum had the answer. She put the precise money into an envelope and pinned it to my coat so the bus conductor could easily remove it from me. She did the same with my travel warrant for the train and I must say both plans worked extremely well, without embarrassment to either party.

I arrived safely in Southampton and strolled down to the docks, safe in the knowledge that I was in plenty of time and would not be late for my shift; in fact, I may be so early that I might even see the Queen Mary arrive. However, one thing had been overlooked. I still did not have my seaman's ID card and without it I would not even be able to get into the docks, never mind board the ship! In desperation, I headed for Canute Street and the Company's Head Office to seek their advice or even get a copy from them – some chance!

Having explained my predicament to the guy behind the counter, who was as useful as a chocolate teapot, I was eventually seen by someone who actually seemed capable of helping me.

A duplicate was out of the question, but what he would do was to issue me with an official letter of authorisation, both for the dock police who guarded the main gates and for the bosun guarding the gangway onto the ship. All this seemed good news to me as once on the ship, I could retrieve my real documents from my cabin. I waited patiently while he went off to get the letter – a ten-minute wait I thought. No chance, an hour and a half later came a young lady with an envelope in her hand, what had she had to do, make the paper/envelopes.

"Mr Aylward?" she asked as she entered the waiting room. "This is for you."

"Thank you very much. Can you pin it to my jacket please as I cannot use my hands," I said waving them in front of her.

"Oh my goodness, what on earth has happened to you? Are you all right?"

"Yes thank you, just a little handicapped, as I burnt both my hands," I responded as she pinned the envelope to my coat.

Off I set, confident in the knowledge that I would be able to gain access to both the docks and the ship. Ten minutes later I arrived at the dock gates where I asked the police officer to read my letter, which he did.

"Just a second, mate. I have never seen a letter like this before and need to speak to the sergeant," and he disappeared into the back office and returned with his superior.

"This seems OK, but I need to send my officer with you to the ship to make sure everything is in order with them," he explained.

So we set off through the docks to where the Queen Mary was docked, the policeman retaining my letter. When we arrived he spoke to the bosun to explain the situation.

"Hang on a second, I will just check," he said.

Deja vu I thought, *surely it cannot happen again*. Just then, Kenny the larder chef, appeared at the top of the gangplank; he had a huge smile on his face and he quickly reassured both officials that everything was in order and I was indeed a genuine crew member, taking my letter, I followed Kenny up the gangplank and back onto the ship.

"Good to see you, Mike. You're a bit of a hero here you know."

"What on earth are you talking about?" I enquired.

"Everybody knows what you did and how you saved Angus from serious injury," reported Kenny. "We will all do what we can to help you so do not be afraid to ask."

We arrived in the kitchen and as we entered, all the chefs started to clap and cheer, which was most embarrassing! Kenny took me straight to the chef's office, where I was greeted by a smiling chef. I had never seen him smile before, it was quite unnerving. He even held out his hand to shake mine before realising that this was impossible.

"Thank you, Kenny, you can get back to work now. I will take it from here. Well, Mike can we get you a cup of tea?" he asked.

"That would be very nice, but I will need a straw to drink through," I added.

The chef sent his secretary off to get a tray of tea and cakes.

"You probably realise that you are a bit of a celebrity on this ship. I have strict instruction to let the Captain know once you are on board, but he can wait until we have had our tea; after all, there is not enough room for three of us to have tea and cakes in this office. Now do you remember what exactly happened because I have heard so many versions that I do not know what to believe?" he enquired.

"I do not really know myself," I replied.

"Right then, we must take Angus's version as the definitive. He said that there was a sharp bump just as you were straining the fat… that must have been when then ship hit the pier, after the Longshoremen cut us adrift. Anyway, it appears that you heroically held onto the friture and even attempted to keep it level, thereby preventing the hot fat from going all over Angus. You even managed to put the friture down before you passed out, but no one knows how," he recalled.

Just then, the secretary returned with the tea and cakes, which he then poured out.

"Would you like a cake? Oh, how will you eat it?" he asked in an extremely flustered manner.

"I would, but you will need to cut it up into bite size pieces. I am afraid I eat in a most disgusting way," I warned.

"When you have finished that, you can telephone the Skipper and tell him Mike is here.

Now where was I? Oh yes. When Yogi tried to take the friture from your hands, he told me the skin started to peel off with it – he even threw up! So they summoned the medics who did remove the friture and took you down to sick bay. We did not see you again until now that is. Can you use your hands at all? Are they still painful? How often do you have to change the dressings?"

Before I could answer, the Captain entered the office; another one wanting to shake my hand before realising the extent of my injuries.

"Welcome back, young man and thank you for your splendid effort the other week, you are a credit to the ship," he said. "I am just sorry that I placed you in this situation, but as you probably know, it was one of those situations which you can do nothing about. I understand that recuperation will be quite a lengthy business and that you are going to need a fair amount of support in the interim. Rest assured we will do all we can to help you. Is there any tea going spare and those cakes look delicious?" he hinted.

As if by magic, the secretary appeared with an extra cup, saucer and plate, confirming what we already knew, he listened to everyone's conversation. The three of us continued with our conversation, which appeared to repeat everything we had already spoken about.

Finally, the Captain left, probably because he had eaten all the remaining cakes and finished off the tea.

"Am I still in my old cabin, chef? And is all my gear still there?" I wanted to know.

"You will have to see your gloryhole steward about all that, as he sorts out all the accommodation issues. In fact, you better go now as he might soon be going ashore. We will see you in the morning when you turn to," he told me; in other words, *bugger off!* So I did.

I spent the best part of the next hour talking to endless new "friends" while I tried to make my way down to my old cabin and the steward. Eventually, I found him.

"Hi, Bunny, do you know what happened to my gear… is it still in my old cabin?" I Asked.

"Sorry, I had to give your bunk to a new student. You should not even have remained in that cabin, as you recently got your rating and so I have put everything of yours into your new cabin ready for you. Come on, I will show you where it is."

I was a little taken aback about losing my berth in the student's cabin as I had developed a good friendship with all the guys who lived there. But times change and I had to change with them, even if it did mean moving cabins. My new cabin was a double, quite luxurious compared to my previous accommodation, as it had its own sink, two single bunks rather than usual one above the other, two wardrobes and a side board each (not just a drawer each under the bottom bunk).

"Who's my cabin mate, Bunny?" I asked.

"At the moment you are on your own, but I do not know how long you will have sole occupancy," he replied. "This bunk technically belongs to the extra sauce chef, if they decide we need one."

"Fine, can you give me a hand to get stowed away, Bunny, as with these hands life is a little difficult."

So for the next couple of hours we spent sorting out my gear and getting it stowed away.

Bunny did agree to take some of my gear and getting it "adapted" with sticky tape, replacing zips and buttons so that I could more easily dress myself and he agreed to pop in in the morning to help me wash and shave. At that time we did not discuss showering arrangements. I must admit that I was glad that I had recently been on leave because I did not have the usual "cocktail bar" in my old wardrobe, only three or four bottles of shorts.

However, I thought, I could soon build up my supplies.

Being alongside in Southampton still, everyone went ashore once they were off duty and so I spent the evening sitting in the Pig with a couple of other guys who did not fancy going ashore. It soon became apparent that I would not be able to drink pints through a straw as I began feeling light headed after only half a pint. So it was then that I decided to swap to Scotch and lemonade, at least I could drink this through a straw without it going straight to my head. Naturally, the evening was a raving success, so much so that I was in bed by nine o'clock.

Next thing I knew was Bunny knocking on my door to wake me up with a lovely cup of tea, complete with a plastic straw (heat resistant of course), and as promised, he aided me to wash, shave and provided a minimum of help to get me dressed in my chef's uniform. Then off I went, off to the Galley to start *work*. True to the chef's word, I was provided with a student who would act as my hands;

his name was Jerry and first impressions were very favourable, as we were still in port it was a gentle induction for both of us. But he did get me a nice breakfast, which he then fed to me.

We did not seem to be producing the same output as I did previously, but I put this down to me having to explain everything to Jerry and his relative inexperienced knife drill skills. The one success of the day was the fact that we did set up a cradle which held a bottle (later filled with Scotch and lemonade, as this combination looked the most like tea).

Naturally, it did not take me long to master drinking from my cradle, although I continued to need help refilling it.

Once we set sail and the pressure started to build for quality food to be produced on time, I became more and more frustrated at not being able to physically do anything, simply because poor Jerry's inexperience and lack of knowledge meant that all his efforts were so slow and not always precise, which effected the end product. As a result, I not only began to drink more, but also, I demanded more Scotch to lemonade and by the end of the day I was positively under the influence of alcohol.

On the third night out, I went to bed as usual – drunk, but this time I fell out of my bunk sometime during the night and the next morning Bunny found me sleeping in the empty wardrobe! When I turned to, I noticed my hands were shaking, and I thought to myself, *God, I am becoming like Kenny*, but that just encouraged me to drink more in an effort to forget. Apparently, I was not a happy drunk and I became more and more bad tempered as time moved on. Sleeping in the wardrobe became the norm.

When we arrived in New York, I prepared myself to go ashore with the rest of the lads, just for a drink you understand, as my bottle was only in the Galley. So off we set, up to US immigration for our permission chit to go ashore. There was the usual long line of crew awaiting their turn so we joined the rear of the queue. Eventually, it was my turn. I asked the officer to remove my documents (American ID card which included my photograph and fingerprints).

"What happened to you, then?" he asked.

So I explained, which it appears did not satisfy him as he called over his superior and asked me to step to one side. A Senior Immigration Officer asked me to follow him to a more private area where he questioned me about the extent of my injuries and why they were bandaged. He too, was unhappy with my responses.

"Wait here," he ordered. With that he went over to the ship's senior officer, where he had a long discussion, presumably about me. The officer went over to the telephone, where he called someone. The American returned to me.

"I am afraid that we have a serious problem which has to be resolved before I can issue a shore pass and so I have asked for your medical records to be brought up. Hopefully, the ship's doctor is still on board and he can answer any questions."

"So what exactly is the problem?" I asked hopefully. "Perhaps I can sort it out."

"It appears that you may not have any fingerprints. If that is the case we cannot allow you to go ashore. Even if you do have prints we most certainly will not allow you to go ashore with your hands all wrapped up in bandages... that would be a criminal's charter," he explained.

My heart sank at this point because I knew I had no fingerprints and neither could I remove my bandages.

"Can I tell my mates to go ahead and not to wait for me. If I do get ashore I will catch them up," I lamented. He agreed and I duly told my waiting crewmates what was going on and to go ahead etc. I returned to the "naughty step" to await my fate. It was not long in before the doctor turned up in person, and it soon became clear that I would not be allowed ashore until my hands were recovered and I had fingerprints once again.

No prizes for guessing what effect this setback had on me. I became more and more frustrated and depressed, which meant I relied more and more upon the alcohol and the trip back to England was an absolute nightmare – both for me and my colleagues. There were times when I could not even turn to because I was so inebriated. Needless to say, my hero status had worn pretty thin by now and culminated in the chef suspending me for the rest of the trip and confining me to the infirmary for the duration.

Once in Southampton, I was taken to the Cunard office, where, luck would have it, I met John, my Union rep, who just happened to be on a course at the time.

"I have just come from a meeting with the personnel officer who has made it perfectly clear that they are not prepared to allow you back on board until you are fit for work again. Obviously, there is nothing I can do about this and so I have to advise you to return home to recuperate. Naturally, you can claim sickness benefit to see you through. When you are fit to resume work, the Union will take action on your behalf to gain compensation for loss of wages and injuries sustained. I worked it out to be around ten thousand pounds (enough to buy three new houses in those days and still have money in the bank)," explained John.

"I will keep in touch when I am in England and will give you a number for any emergency. I will go and get you a travel warrant to get you home," he continued.

"I am sorry but I do not even know your surname?" I said.

He told me his name was John P ******* and I later learnt that he went on to have a successful career as a Union rep .

So I went home to continue my struggle with drink while my hands recovered, but I was lucky, I had supportive parents who quickly identified my problem and had me committed to an asylum (there was no such thing as a rehab clinic in those days, you were simply committed). Luckily, the local asylum had an alcoholic wing and the specialist staff manning it and so my stay was relatively short. At least I stopped drinking.

Because of my drink problem and the lack of National Employment Stamps, I no longer qualified for continuing payments and consequently I had all my benefit stopped, leaving me without any form of income.

Eight months later, I finally lost my bandages and progressed to white lint gloves, which of course brought its own problems for a lad aged twenty. Anyway, at least this allowed me to obtain a job as a retail bread delivery driver, a job I did for a further three months until I was finally cleared to return to work in the kitchens. OK, I had fingerprints but I had no feelings in my hands, which enabled me to take things from the oven without feeling it; however, I was still allergic to the vegetable oil which caused my burns and when I came into contact with it I reacted like sunburn (the skin on my hands would peel).

CHAPTER FOURTEEN

Finally, the day came when I was cleared to return to work and it was with great excitement that I contacted the telephone number provided by John to make an appointment to move everything forward. Eventually, I was able to get a date and time for this meeting. I even managed to get a travel warrant sent through the post for my return to Southampton.

When I arrived at the NUS Headquarters in Southampton, I was shown into a very large and salubrious meeting room where I was given some refreshments whilst I waited.

Within a few minutes, several people came into the room and invited me to join them at the very large table, although I sat opposite to the four men who had just entered.

"Good morning, Mr Aylward, my name is Elliott and I will chair this meeting. Mr Collins is the NUS Legal Advisor. Mr White will take notes of this meeting and you already know John P. The purpose of this meeting is to resolve your claim against Cunard and to discuss your return to work. Is that clear?" he enquired.

"Well yes," I stammered nervously, it all seemed to be extremely formal and daunting.

"Good," he continued. "Now, you were injured as a result of the Queen Mary hitting the quay in New York as she attempted to dock without tug assistance during a Longshoreman's strike. Naturally there is no need to go into exact details at this stage, sufficient to say, that as a result you were unable to work for a period of time and that you received no salary from the Company during this period. Is that correct?"

"Yes, sir," I replied.

"Unfortunately, we appear to have a problem here," he said. "Our records show that you have not paid any Union subscriptions since your injury leave, is that your understanding?"

"Well yes," I replied, "but you have to understand that because of my age and the number of stamps on my NI card, I could not claim any benefits during this period. Therefore I had no income to pay my dues. Also, no one has ever told me that under the circumstances, I had to continue with my subs," I continued.

"Oh dear! This puts a completely different complexion on everything, as technically you are no longer a member of the Union and as such we cannot assist you unless of course you are able to pay off the outstanding amount," he stated.

"But I have no money. I haven't received any money for over a year; how was I expected to make these payments? I certainly do not have any money to pay this off now. Why did no one tell me about this before?" I asked again.

Just then John interrupted, "I did tell you about this before you went home, you remember when we met and I gave you your travel warrant," he claimed.

"Sorry, I do not remember any such discussion. All I remember was your promise to keep in touch with me during my sick leave and the fact that I have never heard a thing from you: no phone calls, no letter, no card, nothing. How do you explain that? If you knew that I was not paying my subs, why didn't you contact me and tell me?" I responded.

"It is not the Union's responsibility to chase outstanding debts; indeed, if you refer to our Terms of Membership you will see that it quite clearly states that 'It is the member's duty to ensure that all subscriptions are paid both in full and promptly. Failure to ensure the said payments will result in the withdrawal of that person's membership', which is what has happened," stated Mr Collins.

"Therefore, there is no point in continuing this meeting as you are no longer a member of the Union and, as you have stated, you have no means of paying off your outstanding dues in order to re-establish your membership. This of course means that the Union cannot, therefore act on your behalf in your claim for damages and loss of wages. Neither can we assist you in restarting your career with Cunard," he stated coldly.

"As I knew nothing about any of this, can I have time to see if I can raise this money?

How much do I actually owe, anyway? If not, can I sue Cunard myself?" I almost begged.

"We could give you a week I suppose. John will you find out how much is outstanding after this meeting. With regard to you suing Cunard, this will not be possible as the Union is a 'closed shop', which means membership is obligatory for employment by the Company and we are the only recognised body that can act against the Company. Any such action can only be instigated if it is on behalf of one of its members," Mr Elliott concluded. With that, they stood up and left the room, not even a shake of the hands, no goodbye or even any good wishes for my future!

A few moments later John P returned, with the details of my debt. By this time I was furious and I am sorry to say that I let him have both barrels of my frustration and anger.

"Calm down, Mike, this will not do you any good; if you cannot behave responsibly I am also going," John said.

Realising my predicament, I got a grip. "So, how much do I owe then?" I enquired.

"I cannot give you an exact figure at the moment, but I can tell you that the weekly subscriptions are based upon your average monthly salary, excluding overtime. This figure can be reduced during periods of absence due to illness. What I can tell you is that the outstanding amount is in the area of one hundred pounds. The office will do a proper calculation and post it on to you in the next few days," he explained.

"That is over two months' salary! Where the hell will I get that kind of money? I am already up to my neck in debt! You really have screwed me up haven't you. All these pretences of being my mate and helping me out was a load of b******t. You just do not know what you are doing. You have ruined my career, you have left me right in the shit, you useless bastard! You better go before I smack you one!" I hissed. Not that that would have been possible as my hands were still not fully recovered from my injuries and they certainly would not have stood up to the rigours of punching someone.

With that he quickly gathered his papers and almost ran out of the room. That was the last time I saw John P.

Needless to say, I was unable to raise the money necessary to pay off my outstanding Union dues and never did receive any form of compensation for my accident or even an apology from the Union, who failed me so badly.

To this day I have never had anything to do with any Trade Union.

How could such a promising career end so disastrously, leaving me with severely burnt hands, no job or prospects and a drink problem? A question I have never been able to answer, even to this day…

Lightning Source UK Ltd.
Milton Keynes UK
UKOW04n0613241117
313240UK00001B/82/P